A Family Affair

A Family Affair

Barbara Riefe

Five Star
Unity, Maine

Five Star First Edition Romance.
Published in conjunction with Sharon Jarvis & Co., Literary Agency.

Front photograph by Tom Knobloch
Back photograph by Gordon Works

December 1999
Standard Print Hardcover Edition.

Five Star Standard Print First Edition Romance Series.

The text of this edition is unabridged.

Set in 11 pt. Plantin by Al Chase.

Printed in the United States on permanent paper.

Library of Congress Cataloging-in-Publication Data
Riefe, Barbara, 1945–
    A family affair / Barbara Riefe. — Five Star 1st ed.
romance, standard print hardcover ed.
      p.   cm. — (Five Star standard print romance series)
    ISBN 0-7862-2138-0 (hc : alk. paper)
    1. Vietnamese Conflict, 1961–1975 — Veterans — United
States — Fiction. I. Title. II. Series.
PS3568.I3633 F36 1999
813'.54 21—dc21   99-041965

A Family Affair

Prologue

"Look around, sergeant, all men dead."

The grenade had knocked Joyner cold. Charlie, standing over him, slapping him, brought him to consciousness. As his head cleared, the insects' monotonous whirring resumed, swelling majestically in the jungle around the clearing. He ducked the swinging hand and struggled to focus. Bowlegs materialized. They belonged to a Vietcong lieutenant, his face as round as the full moon overhead, his eyes as black as a shark's. His English was singsong. He snapped an order. Joyner was pulled to his feet and his wrists bound behind him. His pelvis felt fractured from falling on the two grenades that he carried dangling from his belt. Shark Eyes glared, his brow gleaming as if a light shone inside the bone. He stood with his thumbs in his belt, his legs spread.

"Where you come from, sergeant? Where you go tonight? What you see?"

Come from? The CP. Out on reconnaissance patrol. You already know both answers. What did he see? An ammo dump the size of a city block, weapons by the ton, all brought in by barge up the San River. It confirmed the rumor down from intelligence that Charlie was getting ready to move into the area in force.

Down on their bellies holding their breaths, Joyner and his men had taken one quick look and wriggled backwards out of there. Minutes later Ngo and the other Vietnamese irregular were hacking open a path, a shortcut back to the CP, with their machetes. They'd come upon a clearing bright as noon. Joyner judged it to be about sixty feet across to a wide, unobstructed path on the other side. Stick close to the bamboo and run like hell.

Shark Eyes repeated his questions. Joyner shook away the last of the fuzziness and murmured his name, rank and serial number. The butt of an AK 47 slammed into his kidneys. He fell groaning. Shark Eyes glowered. His men, through looting the dead, came straggling up chattering, laughing. He called to the laggards, hurrying them. Two men pulled Joyner to his feet.

Why spare him? Him alone out of twenty men? Because his stripes made him the highest rank in the patrol. Only he wasn't wearing stripes, nobody showed his rank.

But Shark Eyes had addressed him as sergeant. How did he know? What did it matter? Now he was theirs. What could he tell them? Unit strength, weapons? Things they already knew, only they'd keep pressing, trying for covert stuff, family secrets. What *could* he tell them? He wasn't Intelligence. His eyes roamed the dead. His men, his friends, buddies, companions on fifty patrols like this one. He counted. Seventeen. Two missing. Where was Ngo? Where was the other machete? It had all come down so fast neither could have gotten away. He sighed as it all came clear. Why would either run? They weren't in danger. They'd done their job and walked out. By now they were probably back at the CP reporting the ambush.

"Ngo, Ngo . . ."

One of the men who'd pulled him to his feet shoved him hard in the shoulder, nearly knocking him down again. Joyner ignored him.

"Joyner, Joyner, this is another fine mess I've gotten me into," he grumbled.

"You shut mouth!" shrilled Shark Eyes.

Like a velvety blanket slowly drooping from just above his head fear settled over Joyner. He was their prisoner, to be surrounded by razor wire or bamboo or crammed into a tiger cage. Being taken alive was not a possibility he'd considered back at deployment. Death or survival were the popular options, not capture. It was said that Charlie would rather kill you than feed you. Rice, manioc—cassava root—until you withered into skin and bones, your mouth shrank around your teeth, making them seem to double in size.

The fear cloaking him seeped into his pores. Their prisoner. It would be like being buried alive up to his neck. All his senses would continue to function but he'd be physically helpless, able only to react to what they did to him. And they would force him to do anything they wanted, for a purpose or merely for their amusement. Nothing gave them more pleasure than your suffering. He'd heard the nightmare stories. Now he'd be living them. And the worst they could do to him they would do: keep him alive.

He had enlisted to serve his country. He had come to Vietnam to help save it from the spread of Communism. He had believed that a superior army with superior weapons and leadership could easily defeat the aggressors. He had been certain that the rag-tag enemy would be routed within a year, possibly sooner. He had come believing that he would be the equal of or better than any man he would face in action. He had believed he could make a difference to a beleaguered people, people like Ngo.

He had been wrong on all counts.

Chapter One

Cheryl Forrest Joyner watched as a 707, trailing twisting plumes of pollution, lowered toward the runway. She disliked flying. Every plane she had ever flown on seemed to lumber and fight to stay aloft. The battle against gravity always set her sweating. She stood with Howard in the departure section of Bolton Airport outside Columbus, Ohio, overlooking the tarmac. There was a midmorning lull in traffic. She stared at the scattering of all types of aircraft, empty, unattended, and pictured a giant child in short pants walking in from the horizon, coming to collect his toys.

Howard was off again, this time to St. Louis, for two days. Prospects and old friends in the business were waiting to see him. Everybody in reinsurance knew everyone else. It was an exclusive fraternity devoted to supplying coverage too expensive for ordinary insurers to handle. Howard did well. The downside was that he traveled too much.

He stood flanked by his new attache case and his carry-on bag checking his watch against the overhead clock. He looked especially fit today: urbane, in command, unflappable. Handsome in his new blue lightweight suit. Premature gray streaked his wavy hair, but did not make him look older than his forty-four. He always managed to look fresh, and well-rested, a knack denied most people, herself included.

"That clock is exactly thirty-nine seconds off," he said pointing. "I'm on the second with the car radio, and that was only nine minutes ago."

"Got everything, dear?" He jerked his head back giving her a look that said she couldn't possibly be serious. "Just making sure."

Love in his eyes, he stared at her. "My but you look pretty as a picture today."

"Please, I barely had time to run a comb through my hair. I should have worn a kerchief."

"Nonsense. With your looks, you can get away with it."

Get away with what?

She watched as he moved his carry-on to his other side, setting it against the attache case. They were nearly the same length. Moving the case forward one inch, he brought them flush.

"I wish I could be here when Dave shows up, but I have to go. As far as that goes, who knows when he'll come."

"I thought you said today . . ."

"Hopefully. Time means nothing to him. Last time I saw him he didn't even own a watch. On top of that, it's been nearly two years since he went overseas."

"This is a little scary, meeting my stepson for the first time."

"Relax, dear, you two'll hit it off splendidly. Besides, he won't be around long. Once he starts work he'll want his own apartment."

"Does he know you want to bring him into the company?"

"We talked about it before he left for basic training. We haven't been in contact since his mother's funeral, but that's Dave for you, out of sight, out of mind. Not that we're not close, he's just not the type to stay in touch. Not a whisper from him till that wire yesterday. Keep it, dear. He'll be bringing home pictures. I'm sure he'll want to put them together in a scrapbook. The telegram'll be like a punctuation mark to this whole sorry business. Thank God it's over. No more dreading he'll come home in a body bag."

"What's wrong, Howard?"

"Nothing, nothing. Just thinking about him over there, all he's been through. It has to have changed him. Drastically,

11

don't you think? We'll find out." Once more he checked his watch. "Getting close to boarding." He nodded toward the gates at the far end. "Gate seven. Is my tie straight?"

"Perfect."

He looked troubled. She kissed his cheek impulsively. His eyes flicked left and right. Checking to see if anyone was watching?

"We stop over in Cincinnati coming back. Due in here at five-ten. I left the time on the dresser and the hotel's number and my room number. Tell Dave to give me a ring. Before lunch would be best. On second thought, better not, I'll be in and out. I'd rather our first contact be face to face. You could bring him with you when you pick me up." He frowned. "Maybe not, maybe our first meeting should be at home. Familiar surroundings, you know. He'll appreciate privacy. I sure will . . ."

He inhaled and let it out slowly as if striving to relax.

"Are you worried about seeing him again?"

"Not really. Why should I be?" He looked at his watch. "They'll announce boarding in exactly . . . ninety seconds." He showed her the time. "See if I'm right."

She laughed. "Be wrong. Please. Just this once. Spice up my day."

He was staring at the clock. She eased her right foot forward, pushing his attache case out of alignment with his carry-on. He picked both up without noticing. They walked toward the gate.

"Thirty-nine seconds slow. This is an airport for God's sake. Their clocks should be right on the money. Whoa, I almost forgot, you're working at the library today . . ."

"Noon till six."

"If you have to leave before Dave shows up, leave the key under the mat. A note telling him when you'll be home would be nice. And don't forget to speak to Mavis Delaney about you-know-what."

"It's nothing, Howard."

"You mustn't let people use you." He sniffed disapprovingly. "Making you work the stacks all week like a high-school kid . . ."

"You make it sound like she's chaining me to an oar. And it's only three days, we all take turns."

"She shouldn't just pencil you in without asking. It's courtesy. You give freely of your time . . ."

"I'm not exactly donating plastic surgery. Dear, give it a rest."

"You think I'm being fuddy-duddy . . ."

"I think old age comes soon enough without any help. No need to rehearse for it."

He glanced toward the gate and at his watch. "Now . . ." He brought his index finger down sharply.

"Boarding for flight number three-oh-six to St. Louis," droned the voice over the loudspeaker. "First class only."

He grinned in triumph. She hugged him, puckering her lips for a goodbye kiss. He kissed her. His usual with his usual affectionate but discernible distance from passionate. Over his shoulder she saw a young couple kissing ardently.

"Wish me luck, Cheryl, this trip's important."

"I should hope so. Otherwise, stay home and help me wash windows."

He had gotten into line. She held his carry-on bag for him as he got out his boarding pass. "You'll love Dave, he'll love you." He frowned. "Damn, I forgot to clean his golf clubs for him." He shook his head and lapsed into brooding.

"What?"

"I just pray to heaven he's okay, his nerves aren't all shot. Some come home absolute disasters."

13

"He'll be fine. He must be or they wouldn't have let him out of the hospital. Stop worrying."

"You're right, you're always right."

Seconds later, he passed through, pausing to turn and wave then vanishing into the jetway. She walked back to the parking lot.

"I love you, Howard Joyner. Dearly. We'll stroll together into the sunset. Stroll, not sprint."

Howard was forty-four, nineteen years older than she. Before they'd met she'd never gone out with any man that much older than she was. Never thought about doing so. Prior to their meeting there'd been a succession of men her own age that had almost turned her against men altogether. It was uncanny; every time she got up to bat, she struck out. Friends explained away her disillusionment with the flat assertion that all men are little boys. The ones she'd encountered had certainly lived up to that assessment.

She'd met Howard while on a date with Bill Selby, who worked in the same company as Howard. Over the course of the evening, Bill managed to get indecently drunk and Howard had rescued her, poured Bill into a cab and escorted her home.

She shifted her thoughts from the past to the immediate future. Would David show up before she left for work? She supposed she could have asked Mavis for the day off but it might have been wasted. He might not arrive until very late.

She didn't look forward to this. The instant he stepped over the threshold, there would go their privacy. A stranger in the house, as much a stranger to Howard as to her. And it was easy to see there was no rapport between father and son. Howard implied as much; no contact for four years confirmed it. Did David blame him for his mother's actions? Was *that* Howard's problem?

Twenty-two, only three years younger than she. Would that make things even more awkward? Howard had been too gracious to say so but her hair was a disaster. She fussed with it. It was a shade lighter than chestnut and obstinately straight. Her eyes, her best feature, were a striking blue. Her nose she disliked. It came perilously close to snub and to spoiling her looks. She squeezed the tip lightly as she'd done since grammar school. Hoping to induce what? It always looked the same afterwards.

Would David call her Mom in fun? My God, she'd hate that!

Twenty-two, with nearly four years in the service behind him. Why did he have to come home? Why not pick up his life elsewhere, not automatically fall into the job his father was waiting to offer him? Did he lack initiative? Could taking the easy way be one of his faults? Would he turn out lazy? Would he put off taking the job and lounge about the house all day in his bathrobe swilling beer and picking up his feet, to let her vacuum under them? Howard really hadn't told her a thing about him, his character, his ways, idiosyncracies. Small wonder her imagination was running wild.

His mother had walked out on Howard the week after David was ordered to basic training. Howard had never said and she had never asked why Lydia left him. Two months later word came that she'd been killed in a car accident in Oklahoma City. He had phoned David.

Neither realized it at the time but Lydia's funeral was the last time father and son would be in direct contact for four years. Now home was the soldier. Oh well, he was Howard's son, he had every right to come back to his own home. Maybe she was worrying needlessly, maybe he'd move in and they'd scarcely know he was around, he'd be out most of the time picking up the reins of his old social life. Regardless of that, regardless even of how pleasant he might well turn out to be, how easy to get along with, self-sufficient, neat, picking up after himself, his presence would be disruptive. She'd never been entirely at ease living in Lydia's house, and now her son would be descending on them.

As far as that went, how comfortable would David be with her there?

She straightened the mirror, inserted the ignition key and started the car. Thinking further about David as she got on the road leading to the highway, maybe they'd be lucky, maybe he'd move out in a week, as Howard suggested. Take an apartment in Columbus, to be near his job. That made sense. The three of them could visit every other week or so. Once a month would do.

She loved the *piu lento* passage in the middle of Chopin's "L'Adieu." She must have played the piece five hundred times during her year at Juilliard. It had a haunting quality she found appealing.

She liked his "Ballad Number Three in A flat, Opus Forty-seven," as well. She was fond of all his ballads, but the waltz "L'Adieu" remained her favorite, and the long-suffering and melancholy Chopin her favorite composer. She ended the piece and segued into a mazurka. Howard wasn't big on classical music, though he never quite put it down. Still, he didn't hide his dislike of opera which, she suspected, probably made him feel obligated to tolerate Chopin. He had bought her the white Steinway grand piano for her birthday two years before. She still remembered his expression when he led her into the living room. There it stood with an enormous red ribbon around it. She squealed, he beamed.

The piano was so large and starkly white they ended up re-doing the entire room. The rosewood, mahogany and other

16

dark furniture looked gloomy in comparison to the piano's extravagant whiteness. They replaced the mahogany table near the end wall with an identical lighter one. The chairs and sofa were recovered. Where possible, dark contrasts were eliminated and just enough light colors introduced to reduce the glare of the piano.

Redecorating the living room inspired Cheryl to make other changes. Supplanting Lydia's taste with her own was a gradual process, but someday she would feel that the house was truly hers.

Cheryl was often asked to perform around town, but preferred playing for herself. Chopin and his fellow masters transported her; an audience, even friends, made the journey less enjoyable. She played every day. It nourished her and eased her lingering regret at quitting school and giving up her chance for a "career." Playing also took the edge off her loneliness when Howard was away.

Her concentration wandered, she struck C sharp instead of C natural. She replayed the chord then repeated the passage. One year in New York then back to Holland Springs. How much more advanced would she be today if she hadn't given up Juilliard? Could she have made it? Avery Fisher Hall, Alice Tully, Carnegie, a national tour . . .

She returned to "L'Adieu." The last few bars in particular always struck her as wistful, like the final words exchanged in an unhappy parting of lovers. Today, for some reason, the wistful came close to depressing. The grandfather clock broke in striking the noon hour.

She snatched up her handbag and keys in the foyer and went out. She was preparing to slip the key under the mat along with a note to David when a car pulled up at the curb. The driver got out, coming around and holding the door for his passenger, a tall blonde with an enviable shape. She was chewing gum. In town she would have drawn stares. She had on a light green jacket with brass buttons, miniskirt and spike heels. The driver waved and got their luggage out of the rear seat: matching designer suitcases and his duffel bag, his name stenciled along the side.

"David . . ."

They met halfway down the walk. As they began introductions and shaking hands he stared at her, almost to a point where he made her uncomfortable. Was he resenting his father's remarriage? Was it the marriage or the age difference?

"Cheryl, this is Angela . . . Joyner."

"Surprise," shrilled Angela displaying her diamond.

Cheryl tried consciously to keep from looking too surprised. Angela's smile was warm and genuine but she was nervous. Out of a cavernous handbag she got a tissue to dispose of her gum. She looked about for somewhere to throw it. David lobbed it into the trash can at the corner of the driveway near the sidewalk. Cheryl studied him. He looked nothing like his father. His complexion was not ruddy like Howard's; actually, it was so pale it bordered on pasty. What wasn't understandable was his expression; he seemed to be smelling something rotten. Was he bringing home a packet of problems? He looked exhausted. His brow furrowed questioningly as he eyed the house from one end to the other.

"Green. When I left it was brown, Angie."

"I prefer the green," said Cheryl.

"I thought the brown was perfect."

She snickered to herself. You want to argue? Let's go. She'd be happy to wheel out all her guns and plenty of powder and ball.

"I like brown and green," said Angela. "White is good, too. You were on your way out, Cheryl. Bad timing for us."

"Not at all." Cheryl handed David the key. "I have to go to

work but you can make yourselves at home. There's beer and soda in the fridge and most of a roast chicken, if you're hungry. Your father's in St. Louis on business and will be back tomorrow."

"We drove up from Cincinnati," said Angela. "Davy was getting antsy on the plane so we got off." She looked about the neighborhood. "So this is the famous Holland Springs."

Her tone hinted that she was less than thrilled at what she'd seen thus far.

"I warned you it was small, hon."

He slung the duffel bag over his shoulder and picked up both suitcases, setting them down at the door to hold it open for her.

"Small, quiet, safe," said Cheryl. "Just the way we like it."

"The way we're stuck with it," he added.

Angela brightened. "We can drop off the bags and drive you to work, can't we, Davy?"

His expression was not enthusiastic. Good. He didn't need to do her any favors.

"You don't have to," she said, looking straight at him. "It's only six blocks. I need the exercise."

"Got to keep that girlish figure," said Angela. "Tell me about it."

"How's Pop?"

"Fine, fine. He's dying to see you."

It was the cue for a similar sentiment in response, but he failed to make it. What a nice man. How pleasant, how friendly. It was hard to believe he was even remotely related to Howard. Good, bad, insufferable, home he was. Her stepson. With a wife, no less. No warning, not a clue. Show up, walk in. Take over?

Not a chance. Not her house. Hers. His was brown.

Chapter Two

When Cheryl returned home from the library shortly after six, Angela greeted her at the door. Like a small girl seeking her mother's permission, she asked if she could prepare dinner. She had shopped for groceries before David turned in the rental car. Cheryl gladly surrendered the kitchen to her. She and David sat at the table while Angela worked. He continued to look ill at ease. Did he feel a stranger in his own house? Because she was there? Did he ever smile? In his collection of expressions did he have one that even came close? When they talked, here as out on the sidewalk, she could feel herself frowning because he did. He was aloof, verging on icy, with no reason for it that she could fathom. She had tried to connect with him earlier and again here at the table. Both times he'd shut her out. Not interested.

His problem was obvious. Her, the interloper. He seemed to be trying his best to make her feel uncomfortable, starting with that uncalled for brown and green exchange. He not only disapproved of her, he seemed to dislike her. Let him, if it made him happy. Apart from his unwillingness to be friendly, there was something quirky about him. His eyes looked through her. He was quite strange. Would he tell Howard how he felt about her? He had no idea how they'd gotten together and probably assumed that she'd trapped Howard into marriage. Now she'd taken over his mother's house, sleeping in her bed, in her husband's arms. Extending that further, she'd practically stolen Lydia's life. Was that what he thought?

Not only did he not look anything like his father, they were worlds apart in personality as well. Howard was warm, charming. David was cold, sullen, contentious.

"I love to cook," said Angela. "This is my first chance in months. My cousin Chrissy always wanted to eat out. Restaurants can really go to your hips. You should see Chrissy." She rolled her eyes and tittered.

She turned back to the sink to resume cleaning the fish: Dover sole for the entree. Everything she'd need to prepare the meal she'd laid out, even to lining up the required herbs and spices on the windowsill above the sink. She worked sure-handedly, skillfully, like a professional.

"I like a small kitchen, everything within reach. And oodles of cabinet space. I like your fridge, too, with the freezer on the bottom. It saves so much bending over. And the stove and oven side by side is good."

"Angie was visiting Chris in San Diego," said David. "Chris was a hospital volunteer."

"I volunteered, too," said Angela. "I got sick of sitting around all day waiting for Chrissy to come home. The two of us worked pushing book carts. Don't let anybody ever tell you those carts aren't heavy. That's how Davy and I met, right, sweetheart? He was the only patient who read poetry. It was love at first sight. They kept him there for six weeks after he came back. Tell about the prison camp, sweetheart."

"Let's not get into that."

"He won't talk about it . . ."

"Shut up!" He scowled viciously.

"Who are you to tell her to shut up!?" burst Cheryl.

"I was talking to my wife."

"And I'm talking to you!"

"It's all right, all right," said Angela. Her cheeks were reddening. "I'm sorry, sweetheart," she went on. "I talk too much, Cheryl, in case you haven't noticed. Everybody in our family talks too much, it's inherited. You should see holiday dinners. Do you like to be called Cheryl or Sherry?"

"Whatever you like." Cheryl stood up. "We have Chardonnay. I'll get the glasses."

"Not for me," said David. "I don't drink."

He had fastened his eyes on Angela as he said it. She ignored the hint.

"I like wine, I like how it loosens me up."

He continued staring at her. "I know where the glasses are."

He went into the dining room. Water trickled into the sink. They could hear the cabinet doors and glasses clinking. Angela lowered her voice.

"Anything about the prison camp gets him upset. He doesn't mean anything by it . . ."

"He shouldn't talk to you like that."

Angela raised her voice. "Chardonnay is good. It goes with the sole, too. Wait'll you taste my gazpacho."

He came back with their glasses and examined them in the light. They're clean, Cheryl wanted to snap. It's a clean house, or haven't you noticed? She poured. Angela held her glass with her pinky finger extended facetiously, holding up a wooden spoon in her free hand.

David stared at her. He blinked. Images flipped through his mind. In an instant she was Ngo holding his machete up just before the patrol entered the clearing. He saw his men scattered about. He turned away, screwed his eyes tightly closed, dismissed the impression and looked up to see Cheryl staring.

"Good wine," said Angela, examining the label. "Pretty label, too."

"Howard likes it. I put another bottle in the freezer for dinner."

She looked to David for his reaction. He had none. So he didn't drink, so what? It wasn't as if they needed his permission.

22

Angela brightened and whirled, waving her wooden spoon. "Oooooo, this is going to be a fun evening!"

David said grace bowing his head, closing his eyes. Angela looked at Cheryl, nodding her head left and right. Asking her indulgence? The gazpacho was delicious, the sole, extraordinary. Husband and wife sat across from each other at right angles to Cheryl at the head of the table. The long table behind her was mirrored, even the legs. On it were matching brass lamps with dark, pleated shades. Behind David was the buffet, in one corner, the stemware cabinet, in the other, Angela's left, stood a ball-foot chest of drawers in dark mahogany which had lost its place in the living room when the piano moved in. She could see David continue to note the changes she had made, but after commenting on the change from brown to green outside, he withheld comment.

He raved over Angela's cooking. He liked her, his eyes said so when he looked at her. She came out with inane observations and unintentionally funny comments but he didn't tease or ridicule her. He spared her sarcasm and criticism. His only lapse had been ordering her to shut up. He could at least have said he was sorry, but hadn't bothered. They seemed to be in love. Was it, as Angela said earlier, "at first sight"? Or was it compassion for the war hero? Did women actually marry out of compassion? Was that a war-time phenomenon? It seemed a fragile foundation for marriage.

She thought about her own marriage. After Howard rescued her the night Bill Selby had passed out, she hadn't seen him again for several weeks. Then they bumped into each other downtown and went for coffee. From that afternoon evolved a tenuous relationship which strengthened gradually with each meeting thereafter.

She thought back to her only serious relationship. Two

years older, Tom Patterson was just starting up the executive ladder at his bank. He offered stability and he was caring. Then, less than three weeks before the wedding, she learned he was having an affair with an old girlfriend. Confronted, he confessed and she returned the engagement ring.

It hurt painfully and she learned to be wary since perhaps her judgment was not totally reliable. She met Bill Selby. At first he seemed likeable and dependable. Only he couldn't control his drinking. She never went out with him again after Howard poured him into a cab, giving the driver an extra ten dollars for his promise to wake Bill when he got him home, not just dump him on his doorstep.

She watched Angela reach across the table and cover David's hand affectionately. Angela smiled radiantly. That was love. Would she be able to adjust to Holland Springs, to the people, the ambling pace, the absence of excitement? She recalled her own reaction to New York when she first got there. The culture shock had jolted her. Holland Springs had to be the same for Angela. Had she given any thought at all to how hard adjusting could be?

Cheryl liked Angela. She was a good soul, inexhaustibly cheerful, upbeat. They could become good friends. Angela's biggest problem would be the way she dressed. First impressions could make it not just hard but impossible to fit into Holland Springs. She didn't look cheap; on the contrary, she had about her an air of innocence that Cheryl found endearing. Unfortunately, she looked *too* sophisticated, *too* stylish. The miniskirt had yet to make it to Holland Springs. Angela would be introducing it, in hot pink, no less.

Angela helped her clean up after dinner. To Cheryl's surprise, David pitched in. Howard usually steered clear of the kitchen. To this day he still asked where things were.

Cheryl poured brandy for herself and Angela, then sat

down at the piano and played Cole Porter. Angela sang. Quite well, although now and then she fumbled the lyrics. David played audience. He didn't enjoy it nearly as much but he at least didn't glower and eye the ormolu clock over the fireplace. They had a wonderfully loud time. It was after midnight when David announced he was calling it a night. Angela's cue. He appeared to be suffering from nervous exhaustion. He couldn't sit for more than sixty seconds at a time, couldn't stand for half that long without fidgeting. Didn't seem to know what to do with his hands or his feet.

"Play something classical before we quit," urged Angela.

He nodded. "Play the 'Rondo' from 'A Little Night Music.' "

Cheryl wasn't in the mood for serious music. Not to entertain him. She played it stiffly but Angela cheered and applauded at the end. The best David could muster was a nod of what Cheryl took to be approval.

"Exquisite!" exclaimed Angela.

"Very good," he said. "You're very talented."

"I'll say," said Angela. "I envy you. How come you quit Juilliard?"

Cheryl closed the piano. "I didn't like the city, I felt uncomfortable. I was looking over my shoulder most of the time."

Angela nodded. "New York can do that to some people."

"I wasn't homesick, I just felt out of place. I know I shouldn't have, undergrads came from towns even smaller than here and had no trouble adjusting. Then, near the end of spring term, something happened. Right across the street from Lincoln Center."

Angela narrowed her eyes. "You got mugged."

"Two kids. One had a gun. It scared the daylights out of me. Kids, no more than twelve or thirteen."

"That's New York. If you don't get mugged, you get broken into. I've been both. Like the French say, *c'est la vie*. But me, I looooove New York."

"I left before the term ended. Came slinking home with my tail between my legs." She rose from the bench, "There went my brilliant career." She didn't add that her great-aunt had predicted her failure.

"You really play beautifully," said David.

He surprised her. It was not said grudgingly.

"Thank you."

He was being sincere, he had no idea that it gave her a rueful feeling to hear it.

Chapter Three

"So Ray Schroeder, you remember Ray from the convention, tall, stoop-shouldered. Looks like he's drunk when he's sober. He stands up and says, 'If we take over the Philbin account at a loss our stockholders will go through the roof. You can't keep it a secret. Even if they miss it in the financial page, they'll spot it in a second in the quarterly report.' The only problem with that is he's supposed to explain to the stockholders at the annual meeting that if we don't take over Philbin, Midland Re is almost certain to. It's crazy. I know people who've been in this business for twenty years and still don't know what you've got to do to stay on top. There's nothing unusual or creative about taking a beating to corral a client. It's how you blow out the competition. Then down the road you turn around and cut your loss with other types of coverage. It's a foot in the door, it's done all the time."

She slowed to turn into Chestnut Street. Two boys playing with a football moved out of the way. St. Louis had not gone as well as Howard hoped, but that wasn't what was bothering him. He sat legs crossed, jiggling one foot as if trying to shake his shoe off.

"Relax, dear."

"How did you two hit it off?"

"You already asked that."

"Sorry, I guess I'm a bit jumpy. It's been a long time since Lydia's funeral."

"We're getting along. No shouting matches, no fist fights."

"He must have been shocked."

"If he was he didn't show it. It's been so long maybe he

took it for granted you'd remarried."

"The irony is *he* comes home married. He might have let me know."

"It works both ways, Howard."

"I guess. Did you remember to make a reservation for the four of us at the club Saturday night, the six-thirty seating?"

"I made it. Only why six-thirty? Six-thirty's for the geriatric set. I look around the room and feel forty years older and missing my cane."

"We've been all through that, dear. Eight-thirty's too late, we don't get home until at least ten-twenty, which means we miss the ten o'clock news on TV."

"It's all in the Sunday paper."

"I like my ten o'clock news, Cheryl, you know that."

"I know."

Ten o'clock, switch off the set at ten-thirty and up to bed. On a Saturday night. At forty-four? At sixty-four would it be nine o'clock?

"Did I mention that my plane was three minutes late getting in? How could that be? I can understand fifteen, twenty minutes, but three? The pilot couldn't make up three lousy minutes?"

"Howard . . ."

"I'm being picky, fuddy-duddy, I know, I know . . ."

She turned into Warren Avenue. The house was the last one in the block on the left, the oldest house on the street. In Howard's opinion, the most imposing house in the neighborhood. It had been built in 1927, a small version of a Queen Ann revival clad in its fresh coat of spruce-green paint with white trimming. Under picturesquely jumbled rooflines surrounding a white brick chimney were nine rooms. She slowed the car.

He gawked. "What the . . . what's that?"

She laughed. "It looks suspiciously like a motorcycle."

"For God's sakes! He's not serious. He can't show up for work on that. It's not . . ."

"Well, don't go jumping on him."

"Doesn't he know how important first impressions are?"

As they drew closer David emerged from the garage wiping his hands on a rag. He waved. Cheryl honked the horn. Howard leaned out his side and waved.

"He looks scrawny."

"Angela'll fatten him up. She's a marvelous cook. And very sweet."

"You don't have to sell me, dear. Whatever she is we're stuck with her.

Married . . . I don't believe it. He's only twenty-two. Thank God he'll at least have a job."

She pulled into the driveway. David walked to her side of the car.

"Let me get it out of your way."

Howard got out. "Welcome home, son. You look great. How do you feel?"

"Fine, great, Pop. Look at you, you haven't aged a week."

David walked around to the passenger side. She watched as they stood appraising each other. Howard extended his hand, David shook it. Good God! She couldn't believe her eyes! Four years, not a whisper between them, they come face to face and shake hands. And even that looked forced.

David wheeled the motorcycle onto the lawn. It was black with gleaming chrome trim that was slightly pitted in spots. The gas tank was black with silver detailing. The seat was longer than the tank to accommodate a passenger. Cheryl drove the car into the garage and came back. She noticed that

David, eyeing his motorcycle proudly, failed to see his father's slightly sour expression. If Howard had a fetish it was his lawn. Not so much as a single blade of crabgrass showed. If one dared to pop up, he was on it in a flash with his penknife. Was he worried that oil might drip on the best lawn in the neighborhood?

"A beauty, isn't she?" asked David. "Hasn't been ridden in a while, she was a little slow starting. I just got through adjusting the timing. Hey, don't look so impressed. It's a Harley, Pop, a hog."

"Why a motorcycle?"

"Cheap, easy to maintain, you can park it almost anywhere. Open her up on the highway and she'll clean out your soul like no car can."

"Can we go inside? I could use a drink."

David started toward the garage. "I'll go in the side door and get Angela. She's upstairs fixing her face. Only the fourth time today."

Cheryl and Howard crossed the lawn, the green and perfect mantle of his property, creation of love and labor and constant vigilance. They stood on the walk and he glanced across the street at the neglected patch that passed for his neighbor's lawn. His expression said it all. She held the screen door for him. Inside, David and Angela descended the stairs. She looked gorgeous. Cheryl watched Howard's reaction. He looked slightly stunned.

"Hon, this is my father. Pop, meet Angela."

They shook hands. Howard held onto hers.

"Welcome to the Joyner family, Angela. This calls for a toast. Cheryl, dear, would you get out the Spanish glasses and the brandy?"

He eyed the diminished level of the brandy in the bottle without commenting. He poured. He saw that David had not been given a glass and glanced at Cheryl.

"I don't drink."

"It's just brandy . . ."

"Nothing."

"How come? You drank beer in high school. I remember your mother catching you . . ."

"No more."

Howard shrugged. "Fine, fine, whatever you say."

He toasted Angela, toasted David, toasted marriage. Then launched into a flurry of questions. Listening to him, watching his body language, Cheryl got the impression he was fulfilling an obligation. Questions were expected of him and he wasn't going to disappoint. David pretended interest with grudging cooperation. Howard asked how he felt, the state of his health, his weight, how he was sleeping. When he inquired about Vietnam David waved it away as if dismissing the entire war in one gesture.

"It's good to be home. Holland Springs hasn't changed any . . ."

"He was a prisoner," said Angela.

She caught herself, covering her mouth like a child. Cheryl stiffened. David stared grimly into space.

"You'd rather not talk about it," said Howard, "fine, fine, fine."

Cheryl suppressed a disapproving sound. The atmosphere was getting chillier with every tick of the mantel clock. They weren't comfortable with each other. David was upset because of Lydia. Howard resented David's attitude. The chill intensified.

"How's work?" David asked, breaking a long, weighty, uncomfortable silence, throughout which Angela sat wide-eyed and rigid.

The question was an invitation to Howard to open the

31

floodgates. He declaimed on the company, the changes, the triumphs and near-misses. He started on his trip to St. Louis, only to interrupt himself.

"Before I forget, you two will be staying here of course."

"We've been thinking of an apartment in Columbus."

"Nonsense, waste of money. Rents are ridiculous. And you'd have to pay for utilities and food. Forget Columbus. This is your home, there's plenty of room, you'll have your privacy. Right, Cheryl?"

"You're more than welcome to stay."

God! Why did it sound so trite?

"Okay by me," said Angela. "I like it here, you've got a lovely home, Cheryl."

Howard clapped his hands. "Then it's settled, let's drink to it."

David avoided talking about Vietnam, and at eleven o'clock he and Angela said good night. Cheryl watched them as far as the landing. When she looked back at Howard he was asleep, his empty brandy glass in his hand.

"Howard . . . !"

He jerked awake. "What, what?"

"You fell asleep."

"It's late."

"It's two minutes past eleven. Am I missing something here?"

"What do you mean?"

"Did I get the numbers right? Are you forty-four or seventy-four? Please don't start falling asleep in your chair."

"Momentary lapse. Tough week. She sure is bubbly. His wife. Unbelievable . . ."

"What do you think of David?"

"It's great to see him."

"Is it?"

32

"I wish he didn't look so peaked. And jittery. He used to be relaxed. Like his mother. I remember once a car drove by and backfired. I jumped a foot, he didn't even blink. By the way, did you notice? *He* brought up the business. He's interested."

"I think he was more interested in avoiding talking about Vietnam."

"No, no, interested in Great Lakes. He hung on my every word. Didn't you notice? Her, too. I watched them like a hawk."

"I'm glad you didn't spring the job on him."

"It's too soon, I know that. Give a guy credit. I should buy him a car."

"Don't, he's perfectly happy with his hog."

Don't buy him anything. The way he feels about both of us he's bound to take it wrong. Even the job is going to look like a peace offering, Cheryl thought.

"Like I said, he can't show up for work on that thing. I'll give him a few more days to settle in then we'll sit down and talk turkey about his future. Hey, look at the time, let's hit the hay."

David had been home four days. Howard continued to postpone discussion of the job. Cheryl admired his patience, knowing how eager he was to resolve the situation. She and Howard had just gotten into bed. He advanced the minute hand on the clock to conform to his watch, set the alarm and switched off the lamp.

"Tomorrow's the day. I'll broach it, pin him down. Did I mention that Anson Heeber asked me about him today? It was in the paper that he'd come home. Anson wanted to know when he'd be starting. I told him there was no grand rush, nobody comes home after four years in the service

33

and goes right to work."

"You're worried, aren't you? You don't think David's interested."

He laughed lightly without humor. "You're a mind reader. I suppose I am worried a little because he's changed so, he's a wholly different person. High school seems twenty years ago."

"*How* is he different?"

"His personality. He's . . . I don't know, withdrawn. He's uncomfortable being here, uncomfortable with us."

"With me."

"Both of us. I get the feeling he's sorry he came home."

"What he's coming home to."

"It's like somebody else has taken over his body. A stranger. He's taken on strange quirks. Why is he upset when I say damn or hell? It's just conversation. He reacts almost shocked. And while the four of us were watching the news tonight he motioned to her to sit properly, she was showing too much leg. You must have seen."

"I saw."

"And what's this saying grace when we sit down to eat?"

"There's nothing wrong with saying grace."

"I'm not saying there is but he never said it before. And it's every meal."

"What do you think of Angela now that you're getting to know her?"

"She's a beauty. And very sweet, like you said. Like you, dear, in everything. Just about."

"Now there's a perceptive analysis. She's four years older than he is. She was married before. It ended in annulment. She'll talk about anything, nothing's too personal."

"So I gather. Not too much upstairs."

"Oh, she's not stupid. I like her. Her marriage lasted six

days. She was the one who broke it off. Do you think she and David belong together?"

"Who knows? I don't know enough about her. Him, I definitely don't know. I mean who is this guy walking around inside my son? What happened to Dave?"

"You're exaggerating."

"Not much." He kissed her. "God I missed you . . ."

He shifted the sheet and turned to face her. She kissed him. Moonlight swathed the foot of the bed. The master bedroom was at the end of the upstairs hallway. David and Angela occupied the guest room, Cheryl reasoning that Angela would prefer it over David's old room: no pennants or photos of athletes or rock star posters.

Howard ran a hand lightly down her breast. When he reached the hem of her nightgown he eased it upward. She sat up and whipped it off. When she lay down again she could feel his hardness throbbing against her thigh. She reached down to grasp him.

"Careful . . ." he whispered. "Don't rush me."

She let go. He hovered above her, his gray eyes sparkling with love. He kissed her. She responded, embracing him, rubbing her hands up and down his back.

As a recipe measures ingredients, she could measure the phases of his lovemaking, timing them nearly to the second. Foreplay would last one minute. Once inside her it would last thirty seconds. He would stay inside one more minute before withdrawing, after which they would turn on their sides and lie facing each other again. He enjoyed afterplay more than foreplay, the former to be dispensed with rather than enjoyed. He seemed to think that compensating for the brevity of it after the act was all that was needed. In foreplay he would roll her over and rub her back, starting at her shoulders and working down to her buttocks, stopping when he felt aroused. One minute, measurable by the second hand.

His hands were always warm. When she rolled over after the back rub, he maneuvered between her legs and set himself to enter her. He took it for granted that because he was aroused she had to be. It was a case of ready or not. When she felt his touch down there it was the signal for her to take hold and guide him. He was very gentle, never in a hurry. Gentle, considerate, but to him her enjoyment was secondary to her comfort, he cared most about not hurting her. He was huge inside her. It felt wonderful, it triggered satisfaction comparable to pride of ownership. She held him, owned him, she was in command, he relinquished it to her, if only briefly. He talked during sex. She disliked it but didn't tell him so because it was questions concerned about her comfort: was he too fast? too slow? just right? Her approval assured him that he was pleasing her. In his way, his calculated, methodical, wholly predictable way, he rarely failed to please her.

Just once, just to see if they could, she'd like to go through it from first kiss to final release without him speaking. Don't talk, don't follow the road map, don't be so planned and predictable, put aside the routine procedure—connect the dots to climax—break out of the shafts, go wild, go crazy, surprise me, astonish me!

As he began, his buttocks rising and falling, she thrusting upward, imagination invaded her blanked mind. While she heaved upward mechanically, in her mind she began gyrating, taking complete control, vising him to her, grinding, pulling his buttocks tightly to her with one hand, sliding the other down his face, wetting her fingers in his mouth, trailing saliva down to his nipples. Shoving his fingers into her mouth, sucking, sucking them and rubbing them over her breasts. Thrusting her tongue into his ear, whipping it wet, lashing his face, urging him to do the same to her. Pulling his head down so he could lick her breasts as she bucked and bucked, the friction erecting her clitoris. Awesome, incredible! Clasping his head, grinding his mouth against hers, tumescent tongues battling, bodies writhing in passionate abuse, sweat pouring from them. Hearing him moan, hearing herself as he sank his teeth into her shoulder. And the fierce rush of heat coursing through her setting her trembling. Thrashing his upturned face with her breasts, smothering him with them. Mouths crushing hotly, savagely, darts of sweet fire shooting through her, immolating her pounding heart.

Now she seized his wrists and set his hands to stroking her breasts. Down came his mouth to suck and suck and she squealed with delight. On and on, wild, out of control, rapture, ecstasy until the explosion and the impression of rising from the bed locked together. Then slowly descending as exhaustion overtook them. Touching down, bodies separating, lying back gasping.

Howard was done. As always, he had put his heart and soul into it. For her sake, his own satisfaction was secondary to hers. His cardinal rule. He was devoted to her and to him devotion was of crowning importance, the core and standard of their relationship.

But he always made love the identical way, without so much as a nuance of variation. When they were first married she was tempted to suggest they experiment, but she hesitated. He was satisfied with the missionary position. With his ever reliable road map, he was comfortable. And so generous, so caring, why risk suggesting change or refinement that he might mistake for criticism?

The second hand circled, slicing away thin layers of night. Howard kissed her. His lack of passion she forgave. Passion was, after all, a rare commodity, most people either rejecting it outright or incapable of finding it. Alien territory. She often wondered what his and Lydia's sex life had been like. He'd been younger. Had he been more inventive then? Had Lydia been more skillful at turning him on?

Now there was a purposeless excursion into the abstract!

He had fallen asleep. Smiling. She got out of bed careful not to awaken him. Passing David and Angela's door, she could hear steady, muffled thumping. Angela was moaning, gasping, crying out, louder, louder. She sounded utterly carried away.

Cheryl leaned against the door frame listening.

He'd sneaked out of the hooch to empty his honeybucket. It was raining harder. It hadn't let up for more than a few minutes at a time for over a week. He heard squishing steps. Near the fence two uniformed guards were approaching each other. He'd seen it a hundred times. They'd march up so close they nearly touched noses, halt and march in place like two wind-up toys, execute an about-face and march away. He watched from the shadows. For some reason, this time the routine didn't look automatic. He could sense something wrong. They were nearing each other when Rat, the guard to his right, halted abruptly. Up came his rifle horizontally, he set the butt against the other's chest. They jabbered angrily. It quickly got vicious. The other guard shoved Rat's stock aside and swung his fist. Rat ducked and pulled a knife, plunging it into the other's chest. Astonishment flooded the guard's face as he fell. Rat looked about, retrieved his knife, wiped it on his pants and fled, dragging his rifle by the muzzle.

David tensed, dropped his honeybucket, rushed back inside the hooch and shook Clive Holbrook awake.

"The ladders! The ladders! Get up!"

He explained what happened as Holbrook pulled on his clothes. Outside, he quickly unearthed the rag and rope ladders from their hiding place under the hooch which, like all the buildings, was set on two-foot stilts. The dead guard lay where he'd fallen, the blood washing away in the rain.

"Get his knife, David."

Luck was with them. David tossed the ladder's looped end upward. First try both loops caught on two points of the twelve-foot high palisade.

"You first," said Holbrook, glancing warily about.

The other ladder folded and draped around his neck, David ascended. The third cloth rung ripped under his weight. He hung on and gained the next rung.

"Good lad." Holbrook called up.

On top, David balanced on the third rung from the top and arranged his second ladder over two points, letting it fall outside. Completing his ascent, he stepped easily over the top and onto the outside ladder. Below him, Holbrook was halfway up. He was in poor shape, every rung was an effort. Standing on the outside ladder, with only his head and shoulders exposed above the top of the palisade, David waited impatiently.

"Come on, you can do it!"

Holbrook's crooked grin finally appeared diagonally opposite. He struggled to catch his breath.

"Made it, old boy," he panted.

A shot rang. It caught Holbrook's shoulder, eliciting a grunt as he grimaced. He tried, but could not bring up his right hand. His body swung backwards like a marionette out of control; he would have to pull himself against the palisade to get over. He strained to but could not.

"Help me. My arm, I can't budge it . . ."

David went rigid. He stared at him. Holbrook's body swung back at an angle, the fingers of his left hand whitening with the effort to cling to the point. He hung helplessly, the rain sheeting down between them. A second shot cracked out of the darkness, whining over both their heads. They ducked.

"Daviiid!"

A plea. His tone was desperate. David turned his head away, and scrambled down the ladder. His feet found the soft ground. Claymore mines, capable of sending out between two hundred and four hundred tiny steel balls at a speed of one thousand feet per second, had been placed around the perimeter of the camp. He looked down. It was so dark at the bottom of the palisade, he could not even see his feet. He filled his lungs and stepped into the thick undergrowth.

"Daviiiiid . . . !" He sounded miles away and even more desperate. "Daaaa . . ."

He woke, sitting up wringing with sweat, startling Angela.

"Another nightmare?"

She held him and patted his back. He was trembling, panting, striving to catch his breath. For a few seconds he could not speak then he found his voice.

"Same one. I'm sorry, hon. Sorry, sorry . . ."

She went to the bathroom coming back with a damp face-cloth and towel. They slept naked. She wiped him down.

"Sorry I woke you."

"Feeling better?"

"I'm okay now."

They lay back. He wouldn't get back to sleep for at least an hour. For some reason his subconscious was recalling the escape more often lately, an ogre taking command of his conscience to torture it. Punishment deserved.

"I like your father," she said. "He's neat. Not too stiff. I thought he'd be really stiff. I like Cheryl, too. You should be nicer to her, she's trying to be friends."

"Pop is what he is, a career soldier in the white-collar army."

"You don't like him because of your mother."

"I don't dislike him."

"You resent him, blame him for what happened to her."

"I don't."

"You do, too."

"Maybe a little . . ."

"If that's how you feel what are we doing back here?"

"Hey, it's my home as much as his. It's sure not hers!"

"Ever stop to think you could have it all wrong? Maybe he didn't drive your mother out, maybe she just left?"

"The question is *why*. Only not now." His voice took on a somewhat apologetic tone. "I don't have it in for him. He tries, we've just never been on the same wavelength. It happens. Her, I can't stand."

"Ha. Anybody can see it's mutual. She tried to be friendly, she's given up. I like her. What have you got against her?"

"For one, she's a coward. She admitted running home from New York with her tail between her legs."

"She got mugged."

"So did you, but you didn't run off and hide in Backwater, Wisconsin. She's got talent, Angie. She threw away her big chance because she's spineless. Those muggers did her a favor. She's pathetic, a mouse. You see how she practically jumps and bows when Pop tells her to do something? He'd never dare try that with Mom. She would have handed his head to him. Cheryl's a . . . a . . . she's pitiful."

"She's not. She was orphaned when she was five and had to live with an old-maid great-aunt. She wasn't asking for sympathy. It just came out in conversation. I don't think it was a happy childhood. Besides, you can't blame her for your parents' problem. She wasn't even around."

41

"Another thing I can't stand is the way she tries to protect you from me."

"She does no such thing!"

"Open your eyes. She acts like she's your big sister. Who is she to stick her oar into our lives, anyway? Blame him. Who marries a woman half his age?"

"Just about every guy who can get away with it."

"There's just too much to dislike about her. She's sneaky. I'll bet she listens outside our bedroom door. She's frustrated, she's helpless, she's lazy. She has no kids. Why doesn't she go to work? I mean a real job?"

"She worked. She was a bookkeeper at Clifton something . . ."

"Clifton, Adams and Drury Industries."

"She quit when she got married. She didn't want to. She did it to please your father."

"That's another thing—no mind of her own. She lets him do all her thinking for her. But what really gets me is the way she changed the whole house."

"She has a right, sweetheart. Lots of second wives won't even live in the first wife's house. So her taste is different from your mother's, big deal."

"That's not it!"

"Shhh . . ."

"She changed everything to . . . to wipe out Mom's presence . . . like she's afraid of her ghost or something."

"That's stupid, Davy."

"He's the stupid one, robbing the cradle."

"I know why you don't like her. Because she's sharp. Smart women scare men."

"That's ridiculous."

"I'm glad I'm dumb."

"You're not 'dumb'."

"Hey, with this body I couldn't care less."

"Don't be crude."

"Don't you be a prude."

"I can't sleep." He got up and started putting on his pajamas. "I'm going downstairs. You go back to sleep."

"Is that an order, sergeant?"

"I didn't mean it like that."

"Just go. Dumb people need their sleep, too, you know!"

In the kitchen the stove light was on. Cheryl had brewed a cup of tea. It was upsetting, grown members of the same family pulling in different directions. She didn't like being at least partially the cause. Maybe it was to be expected. What wasn't expected was the breach between father and son. There was one bright possibility. Maybe both she and Howard were worrying unnecessarily. Maybe David would take the job after all. If he did they'd surely get an apartment in Columbus. Would separation heal the breach between father and son?

She sat at the kitchen table in robe and slippers batting the situation about in her mind. Deciding the solution to their problem wasn't up to her, she turned to counting the circle of rivets fastening the vinyl to the chair back across from her: twenty-six. Moonlight slanted through the windows over the sink pathing brightly the black and white checkered linoleum. She thought about Angela. She felt sorry for any woman stuck in a marriage with David. She had failed in her first marriage and was doing her best to make this one work, without much help from David. He was no husband, he was a reclamation project.

"The government should be paying her . . ." Cheryl muttered.

She sipped her tea. David was a mess, and couldn't care

less about adjusting to civilian life. He might be home in body but in his head he was still in the thick of the jungle. That permanent glower: you want to fight? Apart from his myriad of other faults, his spasms of sarcasm, moodiness, restlessness, iciness, his stubborn resistance to friendly overtures, he was a prig. He didn't swear, he shriveled up when anybody said anything off-color; didn't drink, didn't approve of others drinking. She was surprised he didn't lecture Howard.

Maybe she should pick a fight with him. Maybe he'd take the hint and move out with or without Howard's approval. Granted, it took time to shake off the effects of the army and combat, but he could at least make an effort. Another thing, he didn't trust any of them, not even Angela. He was content locked up in his own miserable world. She hated and resented the feeling he forced on her, this walking around on eggs whenever she was in his presence. Don't say anything, don't do anything, don't breathe out of rhythm, don't blink, it might upset him. So he'd been in action, he'd been to hell, so what? So had thousands of others. He was lucky he hadn't come home in a wheelchair, that he hadn't left an arm or leg over there.

The hideous cat clock over the counter ticked away. She had wanted to throw it out as soon as she saw it. Howard, too, thought it tacky, but explained that David had given it to his mother for her birthday when he was twelve, earning the money selling blueberries door to door. So it stayed where Lydia had hung it in all its tackiness. The eyes shifted back and forth, the tail wagged. She frowned at it threateningly. If she pulled the tail off would it ruin the works? She sipped her tea and heard someone padding down the stairs. Howard? Coming to keep her company? David appeared in the doorway.

"Cheryl . . ."

He looked disappointed at seeing her. He had on his old-fashioned diamond bathrobe. The material was lifeless, hanging on him, making him look cadaverous. He looked even more troubled than usual. He started to turn to go back upstairs.

"Wait. How about some tea?"

"I'd rather have milk." He got it out of the refrigerator and took the chair opposite. "You can't sleep either?"

"I find tea helps."

Silence. The cat's eyes shifted, the tail wagged, the ticking so soft it was barely audible. She would be civil, even pleasant, but she wasn't about to send out peace feelers. He felt the same way about her, she was sure. Why else avoid looking directly at her? He seemed preoccupied with counting the bubbles on top of his milk. He had yet to take a sip.

"Your father's going to offer you a job with Great Lakes Re. He's had his heart set on it ever since you left."

"I know."

"You're not interested."

"No. I have my own plans. I want to enroll at Ohio State. That's why I bought the Harley, to get back and forth. I want to get my degree then go for my master's. The government'll be paying for most of it, and I have savings. Angie'll be getting a job. I want to major in religion, with possibly a minor in philosophy."

He looked up from his milk. His eyes asked her approval, at least her understanding. She was too surprised to give him either.

"You want to be a minister?"

"No. I wish I could be. I wish I had the conscience for it. I want to teach religion. Mainly Christianity. Pop'll tell you I'm impulsive, I change my mind like the wind, but I've

45

thought this through. It's no impulse." He paused. She had started on a second cup of tea. "When I was a prisoner I got to be close friends with an Englishman, a civilian, Clive Holbrook."

"A civilian in a prisoner-of-war camp?"

"He taught Oriental languages at Magdalene College, Cambridge. He was on sabbatical in Vinh, in North Vietnam, before the U.S. got involved. One night a bunch of goons broke into his hotel room and took him away. They didn't even give him time to put on his shoes. He was moved from camp to camp. He ended up in Woodrow's Sty."

"Wood . . . ?"

"Woodrow was camp commandant. His real name was Wa Ro. It sounded like Woodrow, all the round-eyes called him that behind his back. Clive had been at the Sty for years when they brought me in."

He was a living skeleton. Everybody was. It was like a Nazi death camp. No point in bringing that up, but maybe he should give her some background. Pop was bound to make a big issue out of his refusal to take the job. If he had her understanding combined with Angela's support, it might help Pop understand and avoid a big blow-up.

"You got away. How?"

"Clive put together two ladders out of rags, discarded pieces of rope, even a knout stolen from one of the guards. We climbed over the wall. I . . . he was shot trying."

"Poor man. . . . Where did you head?"

"West, that was safest. Over the border into Cambodia."

He had crawled only by night, hiding during daylight. He came down with malaria but kept on until he collapsed.

"I ran into a Chinese."

"You said Cambodia . . ."

"But he was Chinese, Zhu Bocheng."

46

Zhu had taught at the University of Kunming, escaping when the Communists overran the country in 1949. Zhu found him, helped him to his hut, located midway down the west face of the Chaine Ammanitique. There he kept goats and grew vegetables and immersed himself in study. At the university his field had been Christianity. Friends had gotten him and his books over the border. On his own he moved down the length of Laos, ending up in Cambodia. Good, good Zhu. He had nursed him back to health.

"I stayed with him for nearly six months."

Luckily Zhu spoke English. In the six months he taught him a great deal. About religion, about himself, opened his mind, changed his thinking, changed his life. Gave it a direction.

"You left there . . ."

"Zhu died. He was very old."

He buried him in the garden. He hated leaving his books but he had a long way to travel, mostly on foot. He hated leaving the goats with nobody to milk them.

"I made it down to the coast. I worked my passage on an Indonesian freighter back up the South China Sea to Japan. The rest you know."

"Amazing. One thing, your father wonders how you got out of the army. He thought they'd put you back on active duty after you were discharged from the hospital."

"I would have gone back except for certain things. I enlisted, I had a good combat record—two Purple Hearts—I was captured, imprisoned, escaped. First chance I got I turned myself in, so to speak. I didn't duck out. I wasn't in the greatest shape by the time they got me to San Diego. I remember a doctor questioning me one afternoon, a colonel. I'd been there about a month at the time. He asked if I'd given any thought to going back on active duty. He had my service record on his lap. I didn't answer, I just stared at him.

47

I couldn't believe he'd ask such a question. He understood. Next thing I knew I was out: medical discharge."

"About the job, let him down easy."

"Yeah. I just wish he didn't have his heart set on it so. He really has no right."

"Right?"

"To take it for granted I can't wait to start. I'm sorry, it's just not for me. You must have seen by now he and I are complete opposites. In everything. How we ever got into the same family . . ."

"He still loves you, David. I know he doesn't say it in words, but he does, and he's damned proud of you."

"He'll think I'm ungrateful, he'll be sore as the devil."

"Want me to speak to him?"

"No. Thanks. We'll work it out between us." He finished the milk. "I guess I'll go back up."

He averted his eyes, pretending sudden interest in the clock. "Cheryl . . ."

"Yes?"

"It's no excuse. And you're probably not even interested but what you've seen so far isn't me."

"So he says."

"He's right."

It was 'no excuse' so why not do something about it? They stared at each other, sharing the sudden awkwardness. All that the newspapers and TV offered regarding Vietnam were statistics, snatches of combat reports, occasional human interest stories, rumors and wild guesses as to when the war would end. Nothing about life in the prison camps, nothing about the effects of combat on those involved. Two Purple Hearts, they had no idea he'd gotten even one. She noticed he hadn't boasted, only citing them as one of the factors that had gotten him his discharge. He stood at the sink rinsing his

48

glass. He started to leave, turning in the doorway to look back at her.

"Good night."

"Good night, sleep well."

"Yeah . . ."

She listened until his steps faded then rinsed out the kettle and her cup. She should read up on the war, pay closer attention to the day-to-day progress, to better understand what was going on over there.

Better to understand him.

Howard came down to breakfast in his gray double-breasted suit accented by a near-outrageously gaudy tie that seriously threatened his dignity. Into the living room he sailed bringing the scent of aftershave lotion. As he did every morning he compared the time of both clocks with his watch. David was dressed for the day and watching the early news. They greeted each other and Howard started for the kitchen. Bacon sizzled in the frying pan and Angela was helping Cheryl with breakfast. Howard stopped, turned around and walked back.

"Dave, what say you dust off your clubs and you and I take a crack at the course at the country club Sunday morning."

"Sure. Only not on Sunday. Angela and I will be going to church."

"That's morning, how about in the afternoon."

"It's still the Sabbath. Can we play Saturday afternoon?"

"Fine, fine. It makes no difference to me." He cleared his throat. "What do you say to coming into the office with me today? I want you to say hello to Walter Havens. Walter's our new president. You remember Walter, he remembers you . . ."

"Pop." David got up and switched off the TV. "We have

49

to talk. There's no point in dragging this out. I'm sorry but I don't want to work for Great Lakes. I couldn't take the job if I did. I'm going to college, OSU. I'm going in today to start the paperwork."

Howard sat slowly, feeling his way down onto the sofa. Cheryl came to the kitchen door, saw the mildly stunned expression on his face, thought better of getting involved and retreated.

Howard relaxed. He grinned. "I get it, you want to study business. That's good . . ."

"I want to study religion."

"Wait, wait, for a second there I thought you said religion."

"I want to teach it."

"Religion. Surprise, surprise. Right between the eyes. What happened, did you feel the call? See the light? I don't get it . . ."

"I'm sorry."

"Hey, don't apologize."

"I'm not."

"It's your life. Cheryl . . ." Howard called. She came to the door. "Can you take the bacon off and you and Angela come in here?"

David threw up his hands. "Do we have to make a federal case out of it?"

"Cheryl, brace yourself. Dave's not going to work after all, he's going to college."

He almost sang the last four words, his expression slightly sour.

"I know," Cheryl said. "He told me."

"So your old man's the last to know, right?" Howard paused. All three waited, eyeing him. "Here's an idea, you go to college. Study whatever. Only night classes. That way you can work during the day. It's done all the time."

"You don't understand. I'm not interested in reinsurance, in any business."

"Whoa, whoa, how do you know till you try it?"

"That's a terrific idea, sweetheart!" Angela had taken David's hand. "Work days, study nights. That way you can have your cake and eat it, too. Or something . . ."

"Or," Howard went on, "put school on the back burner for awhile, take the job and see how you like it. What the hell, you can always quit."

"That wouldn't be fair to the company . . ."

"Howard, he wants to go to college," said Cheryl, so flatly, assertively, the others looked her way.

"This is a critical time for me, Pop. I have to make a choice and college is it. To be honest, business turns me off completely."

"Night courses and work during the days makes the most sense."

"I'd hate it, the conniving, the backbiting, double dealing, sucking up to superiors, scrambling, clawing your way up the ladder, money, money, money . . ."

"Whoa, whoa, who's been brainwashing you? I've been at it twenty-two years. Twenty-two terrific years, satisfying, rewarding. I don't connive, I don't double-deal. I don't make money, money, money. Hell, all I'm guilty of is trying to earn an honest living. And forgive me, call me an idiot, but I love it. I love every day. I'm not ashamed of what I do. It puts bread on the table, it clothed and fed *you* for eighteen years."

"I'm sorry, I guess I got carried away . . ."

"The bacon smells fabulous, girls. I'm famished, can we sit down?"

"Two minutes," said Cheryl as she and Angela returned to the kitchen.

David waited until they were out of earshot.

"You're upset," he said to his father.

"Not a bit."

"You're red as a beet."

"Horse manure." He sniffed. "Religion. You're full of surprises. Does OSU even teach it?"

"Every college teaches some."

"Don't you need a seminary?"

"I'm not interested in preaching. I want to teach it."

"Teachers don't make a fortune, have you thought of that?"

Angela had come to the kitchen door, spatula in hand. "He's right about that sweetheart. I told him, Howard, teachers don't make anything like businessmen. My cousin Bert . . ."

"You could do very, very well with Great Lakes," Howard went on.

"I don't expect to get rich teaching."

"Then you won't be disappointed. I know, I know, people teach for the satisfaction or something."

"Wouldn't it be wonderful if you could do both?" said Angela. "Like Howard said, have your cake and . . ."

"Stay out of this, Angie. Put a lid on it."

Cheryl came out bristling. "Don't you talk to her like that!"

"Whoa, whoa," said Howard.

"She's your wife. You might try and remember that."

"*You* might try minding your own business!"

"Both of you calm down," said Howard. "What is it with you two?"

Cheryl relaxed her glare. "Breakfast is ready. After you eat, dear, go back up and change that tie. Better yet, use it for a shoe rag."

He laughed and she loved him, feeling it surge through her upper body. He'd just taken a blow to his stomach, another to his pride, and he could shrug them off. She felt sorry for him, his great expectations for his only son collapsing in a heap.

Their eyes met. She silently said I love you. He responded, managing a grin.

Chapter Four

Cheryl knew without asking that Angela wouldn't be interested in a job at the library. It wasn't her style, and neither the pay, which was good, nor the fringe benefits, including group medical insurance, would induce her to consider it.

It was a gorgeous September afternoon, the first Friday of the month. Howard was at the office in Columbus, David was visiting OSU, Cheryl and Angela walked into town. They had lunch in a restaurant across the street from Howard's barber shop. Shoppers and business crowded the restaurant. Men ogled Angela's miniskirt, women looked, looked away and whispered to each other. A redhead in her twenties came up to their table and complimented her on it. Cheryl wondered if she did it on a dare from her friends, or if she was struck by Angela's courage. It made for an amusing lunch. They were enjoying their coffee when Angela produced an ad cut out of the classified section of the newspaper. Cheryl read it.

" 'Sales. Alice Bowden's Dress Shop'."

"I know clothes and accessories. I've never sold but it can't be that hard. I mean if you know what you're selling and like it, isn't that half the battle? Look down at the bottom, there's commission, too. Do you know this Alice Bowden?"

"She's dead, they just kept the name. Her husband owns the store. I've shopped there lots. Sheila Ostrowski's the manager. She's okay—a bit neurotic, a workaholic. Very image-conscious, you'd think it was Sak's Fifth Avenue."

"It says there it's on Spring Street. Where would that be from here?"

"Finish your coffee, I'll show you. I could come with you and introduce you to Sheila . . ."

"No. Oh, that's very thoughtful but I should do this on my own. Walk in cold and sell myself. To show her I can sell. I hope I can. How do I look?"

"Angela . . ."

"The miniskirt, I know. We'll go home first and I'll change."

"Good girl."

"It's really stupid. It's the latest thing, it's taking New York by storm. Why does everybody in here stare like I'm naked? On the street, too. Holland Springs, I know, I know. I guess I better cut back on the jewelry, too."

"Maybe just get rid of the necklace and three or four of the rings. And Angela . . ." She set a hand on her forearm, getting her full attention. "If you do get the job, and I'm sure you will, keep in mind this isn't New York. Don't expect to see designer fashions. Women around here prefer to look . . . I don't know, acceptable. We're not exactly Amish, but . . ."

"They all dress the same, just about. Nineteen thirty-eight. Look around in here. Oh, not you, you dress okay. You're not out of it. I mean . . ."

Cheryl laughed. "At Juilliard I *was* Amish. Good luck, dear." She squeezed her arm. "I'll cross my fingers for you."

Angela got the job: five and a half days a week with Monday afternoons off. She came home at twenty past twelve her first day, after orientation.

"Cheryyyll!"

"Up here . . ."

Cheryl sat at her vanity, scissors in hand, holding a lock of her hair straight out and frowning at her mirror. Angela came in.

"Don't do it! My God! Give me those things and hold everything." She dropped the scissors in a drawer. "I'm going

55

back out. Get some magazines. We'll find something just perfect. I'll get you some decent makeup while I'm at it."

David came in around six. Cheryl sat at the piano, finishing "Over the Rainbow," Angela beside her. He gawked.

"Cheryl? Is that you?"

Angela smirked impishly. "Isn't she something?"

"Very nice. Very."

"See, Cheryl, didn't I tell you we won't be able to let you out of the house?" Angela had transformed her. The individual changes were subtle but many and complemented each other so well the overall effect was amazing.

They heard Howard pull into the driveway shortly after seven. Cheryl sat at the piano running up and down the diatonic scale, her eyes lowered to the keyboard. Howard came plodding in, the image of the breadwinner arriving home after a grueling day. She stopped playing and looked up.

"Hi . . ."

He looked up and blinked. "Your face . . ."

"Like it? Angela showed me how to do it. In fact, she did most of it. We got the hair-do out of this month's *Vogue*. You don't like it . . ."

"Dear . . ."

"You don't. It's okay, you can say it."

"I like it." It came out sounding slightly but unmistakably grudging. Conscious of it, he decided it called for elaboration. "It's just so . . . unexpected. You caught me . . ."

"Off balance?"

"But it's actually very nice."

" 'Nice'?"

"Becoming. Beautiful. Yes, yes, beautiful."

It sounded as if the word had conveniently popped to

mind, was appropriate, was what she wanted to hear.

"Or do you think it's too much?"

"Cheryl, it's your hair, your face, it's entirely up to you."

So he said, but it wasn't what he was thinking. He had a stake in this; she'd given it to him in asking for his opinion. He disapproved, only he'd rather not come right out and say so for fear of hurting her feelings.

"It does take a little getting used to," he conceded.

"That bad?"

"I didn't say 'bad' . . ."

David and Angela had been standing by, their eyes flicking between the two of them.

"Nobody's asking me," said David, "but I think she looks sensational. A whole new Cheryl."

New and unacceptable. Howard seemed to be striving to dislodge the disapproval from his eyes; he was succeeding in keeping it from his face. Was it just too much for him? Too severe a change, too sudden? She didn't think it severe, but then any unexpected change was to him. As David and Angela went on extolling her "transformation," his expression became uncomfortable. Why was it too much for him? Because she'd done away with the old Cheryl without asking him, without warning? Was his distress actually resentment, or simply disapproval? Whichever, whatever, it wasn't the reaction she'd hoped for. Maybe he thought she was trying to emulate Angela.

She got up from the bench and came around the piano, kissing him hello. She held his hands. Angela "ahhed" approvingly.

"Excuse me a minute, dear, I have to run upstairs for something."

Out of the corner of her eye, she could see Angela's smile of encouragement slowly fade.

"Don't do it, Cheryl, don't you dare . . ."

She gave her a reassuring smile. Up the stairs she went, conscious of all their eyes. In the bedroom, she closed the door and sat at her mirror assessing her image.

Poor Howard. It was too much to spring on him without warning. Yet it wasn't *that* extreme, wasn't extreme at all, except perhaps the mascara. The way he'd reacted, you'd have thought she'd had plastic surgery. Whatever she thought, or Angela, or David, to Howard it was unacceptable.

She studied her hair and face. The lighting was perfect, her makeup flawless. Her new look. She loved it. She'd never looked nearly so attractive, never had her natural assets flattered her so. The longer she gazed, the better she liked it. She looked stunning!

She felt uncomfortable. Self-conscious? Reaching upward, she unpinned her hair, letting it fall back into the style she'd always worn, the way Howard liked it. Reaching out, she ran her fingertips lightly along the orderly line of jars and bottles Angela had brought home for her, pausing at the mascara remover.

Howard appeared in the mirror behind her.

"I'm sorry, dear, it's . . . just not you."

"I know, it's okay. I'll be down in a few minutes."

Chapter Five

David started at OSU, roaring off on the Harley to his first class, an eight o'clock in History of Religion. He wore the new watch his father had given him. Angela, meanwhile, went to work daily though, Cheryl noted, with steadily diminishing enthusiasm. On her second Friday, she came home fuming.

"Canned!"

"Oh dear . . ."

Cheryl had brewed a pot of tea. They sat on the screened-in back porch. Robins trilled, squirrels trafficked the trees, the dahlias down at the end of the yard were fading.

"Today, the day she fires me, she tells me this past two weeks has been a trial period. I was on trial all this time and never knew it. What a phoney . . ."

"Don't let it get you, it's just a job. It's not like bungled surgery."

"I could smell it coming. You know how you can smell things coming? Bad things? You warned me about the clothes. I couldn't stand them and it showed."

"Did you sell *any*thing? I mean during the two weeks."

"Sure. No. Not really. You just stand there while the customer buys. They pick out whatever, look at the price tag, make a face—always the same face—and say 'what the hell' with their eyes, and hand me the money or credit card. But that's still selling, I guess. Anyway, that's that."

"Cheer up, there has to be a job out there just for you. Open and waiting."

"Today this customer was buying a hat. A brim like this." She held her hands approximately twelve inches from her head. "She asks me how it looks. I told her the truth."

"Oh boy . . ."

"Oh boy is right. That's what I get for being honest."

"What did you say?"

"Oh, nothing insulting, only that the brim was too wide for her, that it made her face look even smaller than it was."

"Oh boy, oh boy . . ."

Angela sipped and shook her head resignedly. "If I knew today was the day I was going to be axed I would have shown up in a miniskirt, no bra and eyelashes out to here. I see by the paper the Merchants Bank is looking for a receptionist. It didn't mention the salary, but it can't be terrible."

"Banks don't pay like stores do, but you're right, it can't be terrible."

"All a receptionist has to do is be friendly and smile and point to the person people ask to see. And answer the phone." She mimed picking up a receiver. "Merchants Bank, Mrs. Joyner speaking, how may I help you?"

"I know Miles Grafton, the loan officer. He and Howard are fellow Rotarians. I could call and tell him you're coming in. Give you a build-up."

"Thanks, but you don't have to. I got Alice Bowden on my own, I can get this. I like just walking in cold. Can I wear jewelry do you think?"

"Some. Just try not to look like you're peddling it. Earrings, one bracelet . . ."

"Go practically naked, you mean. What a town, it's like back in the Dark Ages."

"No plague."

"I should show up wearing a poke bonnet and a straight skirt down to the floor."

"Angela, don't get down on Holland Springs, it has its

good points. Give yourself time, you'll get used to it. You might even get to like it."

"That's what I'm afraid of . . ."

Just before closing time Angela walked into the bank and walked out with the job. She looked striking, and being Howard Joyner's daughter-in-law married to a decorated war veteran hadn't hurt her chances.

Things didn't seem to be working out nearly as smoothly at home. Two nights later Cheryl had given up getting to sleep. It was almost two o'clock by the cat when she sat down in the kitchen with a cup of tea. A half hour later she was on her way back to bed, passing David and Angela's door, when she overheard arguing. It sounded bitter. Angela was still objecting to his choice of careers. She couldn't understand his rigid opposition to taking business courses. Why couldn't he study both business and religion, as Howard suggested? She saw business as a backup, "in case this religious thing doesn't work out." He reacted angrily.

Cheryl eavesdropped until she felt guilty. She got back into bed beside the sleeping Howard. She could see no ready solution to David and Angela's problem; he'd made up his mind as to what he wanted to do before leaving Cambodia. He wasn't about to shelve his aspirations, not even for his wife. Money was the root of Angela's problem. He wasn't interested in money; for her it was important, as it was for any wife. Struggling to make ends meet only aggravated problems. Every wife dreaded financial insecurity.

Holland Springs was the other half of Angela's dilemma. She couldn't have felt more out of place if she'd landed in a foreign country. She was trying but she could no more fit in than Cheryl had in New York. In the meantime the arguing was becoming a nightly ritual, and increasingly caustic. Lying awake, Cheryl and Howard could hear them through both closed doors.

"It goes on and on," muttered Howard. "I don't blame her. I hand it to him practically on a silver platter and he turns up his nose. Anybody else his age offered a chance like this would jump at it. Idiot. Ever see such pigheadedness in your life?"

"I agree he's making a mistake. Only he doesn't think so. And it's his life."

"He's got a wife, for God's sake. He's got financial responsibilities!"

She hesitated to point out that David had a right to do what he wanted in his life or at least give it a try. Howard had said that morning that it was "his life." He had meant it when he said it but he couldn't hide his disappointment or resentment. She hadn't expected it to turn out otherwise. She hated it, but father and son were incapable of connecting. Worse, antagonism simmered below the surface, agreement on anything appeared all but impossible. Even from the grave Lydia was driving a wedge between them.

Why blame Lydia? Maybe she wasn't even a factor, maybe they just plain didn't understand each other. It happened in families. Look at hers. Raised by an austere and distant aunt who rarely acknowledged her existence. Howard and David weren't able to make contact. Neither was willing to compromise.

She wondered what happened on the golf course. How did they make conversation? Was there any? She hesitated to ask Howard. Maybe she should try to make peace between them, but at this stage that looked impossible. Maybe she should mind her own business and not risk making things worse.

When Howard wasn't traveling, the four of them usually ate dinner together. He had just come back from St. Louis again and they were enjoying breast of veal stuffed with anchovies. Howard complimented Angela on it and asked about her new job at the bank. To Cheryl he seemed oblivious to the fact that fitting into any job in Holland Springs was difficult for Angela. Cheryl held her breath.

"The bank's okay. But the people . . ." She flicked them away with one hand, sighing.

"What's the problem now?" David asked with acid in his tone.

"No 'problem,' did I say there was a problem? They're okay, too. They're just borrrrring. They're like zombies. They think because it's a bank they have to be dead serious every minute from doors open to doors close. God forbid you laugh or they look at you like you've spilt something. And now Mr. Hartnett wants me to do his typing. I don't mind typing, but he comes and hangs over me and his breath is like dead fish."

"Mmmmm," murmured Howard. Cheryl could see he was sorry he asked. "How's school?" he asked David.

"Okay."

"Not great? Not even good? Okay . . . ?" He sounded slightly gloating.

"I have to take biology and Spanish One my first year. I don't need either, but that's school policy. You have to limit your electives. If I'd known I would have looked around more."

Cheryl finished the last of her veal. She looked up to see Angela frowning at David? Accusingly?

"You're going overboard on me, aren't you!" she blurted.

He put down his knife and fork. "Here we go. What's the matter now?"

She continued talking directly to Cheryl. "When I was in San Diego, Chrissy went to church every Sunday. I went just to keep her company even though I couldn't stand the minister. You know the type. He'd look straight at you with daggers and pick on you, accuse you. You were damned and you were going to hell, and you'd better wake up to it even though there's nothing you can do to prevent it."

"He made her feel guilty," said David.

"Fire and brimstone," said Howard.

"Reverend Crowder. He thought everybody in the congregation was an ax murderer!"

"You think I'll turn into that?" David scoffed and rolled his eyes. "That's nonsense, you're being ridiculous. He took his religion seriously. More ministers should, more people should. You condemn him for that?"

"I condemn him for ever getting into the pulpit. He was sick!"

"It sounds to me like he scored a direct hit on somebody's conscience."

"You bastard! You sanctimonious pig!"

"Whoa, whoa," interrupted Howard, "take it easy, calm down."

Angela had shot to her feet. "All this crap. Don't drink, don't say boo, don't breathe, your nose stuck in the Bible whenever I want to talk to you. Who are you supposed to be, Jesus?"

She shoved her chair back and walked out. They heard the door slam. Cheryl glared pitchforks.

"So . . ." said Howard, "how are your professors?"

"Okay . . ."

Cheryl got up, "I'll go after her."

"Let her go," said David. "Let her cool off."

Cheryl pointed at him. "Don't tell me what to do!"

Howard groaned, "Hey, don't you two start . . ."

"My wife's self-appointed protector is upset with me. Again."

"She could use protection!"

She started after Angela. It was coming to a head. It had

to, they'd reached the stage where they couldn't stand each other. The looks at the table confirmed that. Angela wasn't to blame for any of it. She was a neglected wife, a wife whose input he ignored completely. He gave her no say in anything. Her opinions were worthless. In effect, he'd stripped her of her marriage rights.

Why didn't he leave? How can anybody stay where they know they're not wanted? Columbus would be much better for Angela, too. She'd have a whole range of jobs to choose from, and she'd be happier there. It would do them both good, not that she cared about him.

"Sanctimonious pig . . ."

Talk about hitting the nail on the head. Angela was out of sight by the time Cheryl got to the sidewalk. She must have run. There was no telling in which direction she'd headed. Maybe he was right. Maybe it was better she left, give them both a chance to cool off. Cheryl went back inside. They finished dinner in silence. Angela came back two hours later. She apologized to Cheryl and Howard. She didn't even look at David. That night the recurring argument degenerated into shouting, waking Cheryl and Howard.

"Hold onto your hat, here we go again." Howard rose on one elbow and rubbed his eyes. "It's every night. How's anybody supposed to sleep? Listen, they're really going at it this time. Should I go break it up?"

"Don't you dare!"

They heard the door slam and stomping down the hall, down the stairs.

Howard grunted. "Watch, tomorrow night he'll be back sleeping in his old room. She should stop beating a dead horse, she'll never change his mind."

"Everything's falling apart on her lately. She's desperately unhappy."

"The glow is off the rose."

"It's not funny. I feel sorry for her, she can't handle any of this."

"You mean his going to college . . ."

"College, Holland Springs, Ohio against New York, the dress shop, the bank, everything. She's miserable."

"She said that?"

"She doesn't have to, she can't hide it. For somebody normally so happy, it's criminal!"

"Listen, he's coming back up. Round two . . ."

They heard the bedroom door open and close. The fight did not resume.

David had morning classes. He returned to Holland Springs early in the afternoon, parking the Harley in front of the glass-doored entrance to Somerset Apartments in town and starting up the street to the drug store. A woman called him.

He turned and saw Jackie Strayhorne, a beautiful redhead with a shape to rival Angela's, an old girlfriend from high school.

"Davy . . . !"

"Hi, Jackie . . ."

Her name had been Strayhorne until late in their senior year. When David and Jackie broke up, she started going with Brady Coomes, the mayor's son. They got married a few weeks before graduation. David and Brady had been friends until Brady moved in on Jackie, then a wall went up between them. It came down shortly after graduation, and together they went to the induction center in Columbus to join the army. David considered himself patriotic; Brady suffered a patriotic seizure. A second affliction was his downfall: it turned out he had a heart murmur. He was rejected.

Jackie's seductive green eyes stared at David, eating him up. "Davy, Davy. I heard you were home, with a new wife and everything."

"Everything. You look sensational, Jackie."

"You, too, yum, yum."

"How's old Brady?"

"Old Brady is good. You know Brady, he just sort of putters along."

"Is he still with the power company?"

"Forever."

"You live here in the Somerset?"

"Third floor. Hey, Brady's off today, come on up and say hello. Tell us about Vietnam. Everything he missed." She took his arm. "Come on, Davy, surprise him. For old time's sake."

"Old time's sake, sure."

She led the way up the stairs. The hallways smelled of disinfectant. The window at the end of the third floor was opaque with grime. She got out her key to unlock the door which struck him as odd—why would Brady lock himself in? When she stood aside to let him in he blinked at the disarray. The front room was a mess. The wallpaper was shabby and peeling in a number of places, the place smelled of stale beer. Looking through to the kitchen, he could see a section of the counter crowded with dirty dishes. She pushed a newspaper off the sofa onto the floor.

"Sit, sit . . ."

"Where's Brady?"

She covered her mouth, one hand over the other. "I'm bad. I lied, he's not here. I threw him out two weeks ago. I got sick of living with an alcoholic."

"Brady? He never even touched beer, he was always in training."

"He still is. For the Drunk of the Month Club. He's a lush. I've had it with him." She was standing to one side looking down at him. She ran the tip of her tongue across her upper lip. "Yum, yum."

He shifted uncomfortably. She had on a tight sweater with no bra. Her skirt came to just above her knee. She continued ogling him, tossing her flaming red hair. She ran her fingers through it and, lifting her leg, set her foot on the arm of the sofa to retie her sneaker, making sure she was positioned so that he had a clear view all the way up to her crotch. She wore no panties. He looked away.

"Jackie . . ."

"Oh, shame on me!"

"I have to go."

He started to get up. She leered and pushed him back down. Then her expression darkened, became sad.

"Please don't go yet. We haven't seen each other in ages. You look sensational. Delicious. Yum, yum."

Before he could respond, she sank to her knees in front of him and reached out.

Cheryl had a hard time keeping her mind on her work. She was too full of Angela and her problems. Her marriage was deteriorating into a struggle for survival.

Cheryl left the library in the middle of the afternoon to pick up wine at the liquor store and stop in at the bank to say hello to Angela. She was passing Howard's barber shop when she spotted David's Harley parked across the street. She looked for him in the vicinity. The oval glass door to the Somerset Apartments caught the sun as it opened and out came the same stunning redhead who had complimented Angela on her miniskirt in the restaurant the day she applied for the job at Alice Bowden's. Cheryl's jaw sagged as David came out behind the woman. She watched as the redhead turned, took David's arm and rested her head on his shoulder. As she did so, David recognized Cheryl and waved.

Stung by his brazenness, she stared. She started back up the street toward the library. Forget the wine, the bank . . .

"Cheryl!"

She pretended not to hear. The bastard! Contemptible pig! Sweet, loyal, faithful Angela, working to support them in a job she couldn't stand, and this was the thanks she got!

"Pig. Pig!"

Cheryl finished work and came home shortly after six. Angela was in the kitchen. Cheryl could hear dishes and utensils being moved about. She could barely distinguish David's voice. He was sitting at the table out of sight. Angela called to her and she responded. She heard a chair scrape the floor. David came to the doorway. At sight of him, revulsion lumped Cheryl's throat. He didn't even have the decency to look embarrassed.

"Hi," he said.

"Hello."

She fought the urge to march past him and confront Angela, blurt it out right in front of him. Angela had a right to know. Still, she had enough to contend with without Cheryl adding to it. It would devastate her, she'd go wild, she'd probably attack him.

Cheryl sighed and turned her back on them. The fragility of the situation had to be taken into account, only by not telling Angela she'd be condoning it. Why protect him? On the other hand, why tell? So she could gloat over the embarrassment it caused him? For the amusement of watching him try to explain it?

69

No. As distasteful as it was, as undeserving as he might be, she should give him the chance to own up to it. He might, out of fear that she'd tell Angela first.

"I'll give you a hand with dinner, dear," she called. "First give me a minute to freshen up."

She went upstairs. She was at the bathroom sink rinsing her face when David appeared in the open doorway.

"It was nothing, Cheryl, I swear. Nothing happened."

"Get away from me."

"She's an old girlfriend from high school. She's married for God's sake. She asked me to come up to her apartment. She said her husband was up there. Brady Coombs. He and I used to be buddies . . ."

"I don't want to hear. If you want to tell somebody, tell your wife."

"Cheryl . . ."

"Leave me alone!"

She slammed the door in his face and stood listening until she heard his footsteps fade. Good! Damned if she'd let him unburden his miserable conscience on her and ignore his wife. Cheryl despised him.

"Pig!"

For the next several days Cheryl kept silent. As David did, as he must have, there was no explosion between husband and wife. With so much time having elapsed he probably never would tell her. Was he gambling that she wouldn't tell Angela either?

For Angela's sake she tried to be polite, keeping on a frozen smile. David behaved the same way toward her, but Howard sensed something was wrong. Cheryl denied it, so convincingly he finally let the matter drop.

Her contempt for David smoldered. What he did and with

whom she couldn't have cared less. Angela was her concern. She tried so hard to make the marriage work, giving and getting so little in return. Lately, all he did was feed her unhappiness.

She was infuriated with David's attitude, as if he'd done nothing. His head crammed with religion, "thou shalt not covet they neighbor's wife" evidently didn't fit into his moral code. Disgusting hypocrite!

At noon on Thursday, nearly two weeks after Cheryl saw David with his friend's wife, Howard left for Omaha for a two-hour meeting, returning that evening. David had late classes, ending the day with a three-hour biology lab. Cheryl had the day off. She came home with groceries around 2:30 to find Angela's suitcases by the door. She sat with her chin on her hands staring at the clock.

"I'm leaving him, Cheryl. I quit my job, I'm going back to New York."

"Did he tell you about . . ."

"What?"

"Nothing. It's not important. Another job possibility for you."

"It's a little late for that. Tell him he'll be hearing from my lawyer. Marriage number two down the tubes. I left him a letter. I don't want anything, only out."

"Angela . . ."

"Please don't try and talk me out of it. It's the only way. No big deal, that's life. Lots of marriages don't work out. Mine never do."

"Can't you at least wait till he gets home? Sit down and discuss it?"

"What for? We'd both have to have horse blinders on not to see it's over. Besides, my plane leaves at ten of four. I didn't know when you'd be home so I called a cab."

"This is crazy . . ."

"The letter's on the bureau. Cheryl . . ." She smiled thinly at her. "You've been super to me. Thank you for all your help. Anybody with you for a friend is the luckiest person in the world. It's funny, I'm a year older than you but I feel like you're my big sister. I wouldn't have lasted this long if it hadn't been for you. Howard's nice, too. Sweet. And he's got his head screwed on right, not like some people. He's honest, too. He never says something that means something else. Tell him I said good-bye. In case you wonder, the answer is yes— even with everything I still love Davy. That's what's making this so hard. I'll miss him."

"Don't go, Angela. Please . . ."

"Really miss him. In bed when we're not fighting I can't get enough of him. But then all our problems fall on us, like a ceiling collapsing. Wouldn't it be perfect if we never had to get up?"

She sniffed and averted her eyes. Cheryl closed her hand over Angela's.

"Our trouble is we didn't look ahead far enough. I didn't. It's not as if he tried to keep it a secret. I just didn't think about it. I was too wrapped up in him."

"You held up your end, dear, you were a good wife. The best."

"I tried. Honest. Believe it or not, I hate this. Walking out on somebody you love is not easy, but I just can't deal with it. It's crushing me to death. Oh, it's not like I thought every-thing was going to be dandy forever, like back in California. I just never expected this—this town, this life is prison, like the camp was to Davy. I'm not leaving, I'm escaping. The town's not the worst of it, it's what he wants to do with his whole life! Not the teaching part, that's okay, I guess. Except Howard's right, the money stinks. What scares me is the religion."

"Scares you? How?"

"I think some people, I mean the ones who wrap themselves up in it like he's doing, get in over their heads. They can't handle it. I'm scared it'll change him into a whole different person. It's already starting, and I don't want to be around to see how it ends, how he does. People *get* religion all the time. That's okay, only a lot turn into Reverend Crowder. They don't take it on, it takes them. Listen to me spout. Am I making sense?"

"Of course you are. Only the big thing is the money, isn't it? The job."

"You bet it is. Howard as good as hands him a fortune, his whole future, all that, that . . ."

"Potential."

"That's the word. And he turns his back on it. You know money is terrifically important. You don't know, you don't have to worry about it. But it makes all the difference in the world as to how you live. If you're always broke you're at each other's throats, scrimping, eating lousy, wearing cheap clothes, everything in the house falling apart and you can't afford to fix it. Is it so terrible of me to want security? A wife needs security almost as much as she needs love. The worst of it is she has no control over it. She depends on the man. And he, Davy, doesn't care beans about it."

"Shhhh, don't get upset."

"Am I wrong? Am I being greedy?"

"Not at all. Practically every wife has the same fear."

She squeezed Cheryl's hands. "You are something, so easy to talk to. Howard's so lucky."

"Angela, we've still got time. When your taxi comes, send him away, we'll talk."

"Please, that'll only make it harder. You could talk me

73

into staying but it'd still be wrong."

"Every married couple experiences rough periods. Howard and I do."

"This isn't any 'rough period.' It's our whole life together. He's just getting started and already I'm sick to death of hearing about religion. He can change the world without me around. Besides, he knows I'm leaving, he won't be surprised."

"You told him?"

"No, but he knows. He just doesn't know when. Face it, we've been going downhill ever since Alice Bowden. I'm not blaming him, I'm not blaming me. It's . . ."

A horn sounded outside. "That's my cab."

She kissed Cheryl and held her. "Don't cry."

Cheryl turned her toward the foyer mirror. "Look who's talking."

"That's just ragweed. Well, maybe a little crying. Please, don't you. I'll cry all the way to the airport and ruin my makeup. One last thing, and I really believe this. Honestly. For what he wants to do, he's better off without me."

"You're wrong."

"I'm not. Deep down he knows."

"I'll miss you terribly. Will you write?"

"I can't. Then it wouldn't be a clean break. I'll miss you, too, Cheryl. I'll miss you playing and me trying to sing, our lunches, all our girl talk. It's been fun, it's what's held me together this long. You're a good friend. He's honking . . ."

Cheryl kissed her. "Take care of my sister. She's precious goods."

"Sister, I like that. Don't come out. I'll fall apart if you come out. We'll say good-bye here, okay? Good-bye . . . Sis."

She ran out to the cab and was gone. The tires squealed around the corner. Cheryl closed the door, went to the piano and played the opening bars of *Anything Goes* with one finger. Then she went to her handbag for a tissue.

She thought about Angela, about herself, and what they'd said. Why had she tried to talk Angela into staying? As painful as it was, wasn't she better off leaving him? He'd cheated once and gotten away with it, what better incentive than to keep on cheating?

"Better off. She is better off."

Chapter Six

Cheryl was emptying the dishwasher when she heard the Harley roar into the driveway.

"Here we go . . ."

It would shatter him but he was to blame. He'd asked for it, he deserved it. He wasn't worthy of a woman as loving, loyal and unselfish as Angela. Wasn't worthy of any woman, wasn't marriage material. There was one bright spot: with Angela gone he probably wouldn't stay, not with this breach with his father. Not with the way they felt about each other. He was singing when he came through the garage door.

"Hi . . ."

"Hello."

"Angie around?"

"You'd better sit down."

"What's wrong?"

His face darkened, he seemed to tense. If she hadn't known him so well, she might feel sorry for him. He sat and she told him. It seemed to paralyze him. He said nothing only pursing his lips oddly, furrowing his brow, staring into space. Then he began to jiggle one leg, the way Howard did when he was nervous.

"She left you a letter on the bureau."

He got up without speaking and headed for the stairs. He started up, pausing on the fourth step.

"Will you come up?"

In the bedroom, while he read the letter to himself, she glanced around. His Bible lay on the night stand. A copy of Christina Rossetti's poems lay open facedown on the bureau. He was through reading the letter. Still no comment. Why ask her to come upstairs if he didn't want to discuss it with her? For moral support? He read the letter through a second time on the way downstairs.

They sat in the kitchen. A third time he read the letter then set it in front of him and squared the pages neatly. Why didn't he crumple it, throw it away? Why was he so calm? Was he absorbing the full impact before deciding which emotions to show. His eyes stayed on the letter as he finally spoke.

"Well, this is another fine mess I've gotten me into . . ."

"You think it's funny?"

"Do I look as if I do?"

"I'm sorry, but you get no sympathy from me."

"*I'm sorry,* I haven't heard me ask for any."

"You could have been honest, you could have told her you cheated on her. You just didn't have the guts."

"I didn't tell her because I didn't do anything."

"Of course not."

"Jackie lied. She told me Brady, her husband, my old buddy from high school, was upstairs in the apartment. I went up with her. He wasn't there, she tried to come on to me, I left."

"Good for you."

"Nothing happened."

"I saw you clinging to her on the sidewalk."

"No, you didn't, you saw *her* clinging to me. Jackie loves to hang on." He stared icily. "You just have to believe I'm lying, don't you? I cheated on Angie. Why bother to check? You could. You could ask Jackie. Can you handle the truth if she tells it to you, that I never touched her?

"I hate to disappoint you, Cheryl, but tomcatting around isn't my style. I take after my father. Too bad Angie's not here, she could tell you." He was staring at her, his eyes suffused with indignation. He was telling the truth. She sensed it intuitively. Like a double-throw knife switch thrown the opposite way, the sincerity in his face, his tone, wiped away her suspicion. He laughed thinly. "On second thought, you don't have to believe me. Why should I care what you think? And what difference does it make now, right? Only you might ask yourself what exactly did you see? Coming out of the Somerset with her, did either of us look disheveled? Turned on? Basking in the glow? Were we falling all over each other? What?"

"It . . . was a shock seeing you with her."

"So you jumped to conclusions. Knowing how fond you are of me, how trusting, it figures. Do it Cheryl, ask Jackie. Until she straightens you out, can we drop it? I've suddenly got something a little higher in priority here."

So he was innocent. The way he was staring at her made her shrink slightly.

"I asked for this. I just wish we could have sat down and thrashed it out."

He raised his face. Cheryl looked over at the half-emptied dishwasher. The pain in his eyes was disturbing.

"She didn't think discussing it would help any," she murmured.

Something stirred inside her. Sympathy? More like maternal instinct. He wasn't a grown man home from the wars, he was a boy who'd been grievously hurt. He was suffering. She suddenly wanted to console him. He needed help. What ailed her?

"It was past that." He rose from his chair and turned to grip the edge of the sink. "I'm going after her. Apologies, pleas, hat in hand. There can't be too many Ohlsons in the Manhattan phone book. Her father's name is Sven." They heard the front door open. He turned from the sink bursting into a radiant smile, instantaneous relief. "Angie!"

Cheryl looked up at the cat swinging its tail, shifting its eyes. "No, it's Howard. He got a ride from the airport with Everett Cutler. They're home from Omaha."

Skepticism narrowed his eyes. "It's Angie . . ."

"Hi, dear," Howard called from the living room.

Angela's letter was still on the table. She folded it and put it in the note rack under the wall phone.

"Better mix him a drink," said David. "He's going to need it."

He looked like a wall had collapsed on him. She recalled Angela telling her that her leaving would be no surprise to him. She was wrong. And now, too late, he proved he loved her. For all his faults, his neglect, his patronizing attitude, his indifference to her needs and feelings, he loved her. It seemed a blatant contradiction but there it was. Loved her, lost her and it was devastating him.

Howard came in. He kissed her and greeted David. She went to fix him a martini, leaving them in privacy. David's voice as he told him was barely audible. She heard Howard's "No!" as she returned to the kitchen with his drink.

David looked about. "Where's the phone book, Cheryl? I have to call the airport, find out about flights to New York."

"You're not going after her . . . ?" Howard frowned. "Don't. Give it up."

"He's right," said Cheryl. Her bluntness stopped David's searching. She could have told him she'd moved the phone book to the drawer beneath the silverware. "It's over, she was very clear about that. Clear and adamant."

He weighed this as he sat slowly. "I'm to blame for everything. For bringing her here in the first place, instead of settling in Columbus. In the city we'd have gotten off to a better start. Seen more of each other. And she'd have liked it there. She wouldn't have had to contend with Holland Springs." He looked up at one then the other. "I'm rambling, this is embarrassing."

"Don't blame yourself," said Howard. "She left you, not the other way around."

Cheryl sighed to herself. David didn't seem to hear him.

"I saw it coming when we drove into town, her expression when she looked around, but I paid no attention. That's another thing, I never did pay much attention. She wouldn't have hung around this long if it hadn't been for you, Cheryl. You made it tolerable for her. She appreciated it, she loved you, you're the one she'll miss."

"David . . ."

"Well, we tried. She did. She needed attention. I don't mean she craved it, but she did need it, being in a strange place. I was too busy, I let things get in the way. The glow was fading. It was the time we should be cementing our relationship. Instead, I let it trundle along on its own."

"You just have to take the blame, don't you!" snapped Howard.

"Who am I supposed to blame?"

Howard sipped his drink. Cheryl pretended to concentrate on the dishwasher again, avoiding looking at David. Gone was the lost look, the embarrassment. Suffering was setting in. She tried to ease some of the blame onto Angela, but she could not.

"Where the devil is that phone book?" he burst.

"Forget it," advised Howard. "Calm down and think about it before going off half-cocked. You'll get to New York, you'll find her, you'll sit down and try to thrash it out. Good, fine, only what makes you think you'll talk her into coming back? Not to Holland Springs, you won't. Even I could see she hated it here. You think she had a change of heart over Pittsburgh? Her plane's landed by now, she would have phoned from the airport."

David said nothing for a full minute. The cat's tail swung. He seemed to be mulling over Howard's words. Howard watched and sipped. Staring at the dishwasher, Cheryl felt ridiculous, as if she were trying to empty the rest of the dishes telekinetically. Her heart softened. Her feelings surprised her. She did feel sympathy for him. He wasn't whining or asking for sympathy. If he felt self-pity, he gave no sign. He had yet to criticize Angela. He was concentrating on trying to come to terms with it.

How was Angela? Any delayed reactions? Second thoughts? None that moved her to pick up a phone. She'd never see Angela again. A friend had dropped out of her life. No calls, no contact, not even Christmas cards. A friend irretrievably lost, unless she went with Howard on a business trip to New York. That had happened only once since they were married. Still, there was always the chance. If he did go again, she'd go along, find Angela, they'd sit and talk. Then what? Part a second time? What would that accomplish?

Sympathy for David had rooted and was growing. He'd lived a lifetime in two years in southeast Asia. Come home, fallen in love, married, started over, started putting the prison camp behind him, college . . . now this.

Howard had been detailing the reasons David should not run after Angela. He meant well but it was overkill. David's expression said so. He'd already decided against it. *Drop it, dear.*

In bed waiting for sleep, Cheryl wondered if David was able to get to sleep. Were his thoughts and his conscience still churning? By the time the three of them called it a night, he seemed to be accepting it, or at least bearing it. She pictured him lying on his back, his hands behind his head, staring at the ceiling, heaping coals on himself. Nothing either she or Howard could say would discourage that. Did he fault their failure to locate somewhere in Columbus? Going to college instead of taking the job with Great Lakes Re? There had to be something badly out of kilter to have to jettison your dream in order to preserve your marriage. He'd have been miserable working in reinsurance.

"You know," said Howard, breaking into her thoughts, "if he'd taken the job she never would have left, none of this would have happened."

"I know, I know, but he didn't and she did."

"He can blame himself."

"Leave him alone, Howard, please."

"Whoa, whoa, what is this? You two can't stand each other."

"I . . . feel sorry for him. So should you."

"I do, I'm simply stating a fact. If he took the job . . ."

"Oh, will you stop it with the job!"

"All right, all right."

"Angela left because she couldn't deal with his problems."

"Not to mention her own. And he was no help."

"Because of the condition he's in. He's only semi-readjusted, if that far. He needs both of us, Howard, not to pamper him or fall over him with sympathy, just to be . . . patient."

"Understanding."

"Right."

"Hey, I play golf with him every Saturday, we talk, we're both trying. We're just, I don't know, oil and water. That's the way it is with some families. I'm not finding fault, just stating a fact. It's the goddamn war."

It was and it wasn't. She didn't particularly want to prolong a discussion of it. Howard was trying, maybe they'd become closer, maybe Angela's leaving would help.

Four days later David came home from morning class and offered Cheryl a ride to the library on the Harley.

"Thanks but no thanks. People will gawk and snicker and when Mavis Delaney hears us roaring up she'll look out the window and have a kitten on the sill."

"So I let you off a block from the library. Come on, Cheryl, give it a try. You can wear Angie's helmet, tuck your hair up, dark glasses, nobody'll know it's you. It's fun, you'll see."

"Maybe some other time."

"Please, just try it. Just once. You'll love it. You've never ridden on one, have you?"

"Never had the desire to."

"It's time. I'll keep bugging you till you give in. Angie loved it, you will, too. If you don't, I promise I'll never ask you again. Come on, burst out for once."

"Out of what?"

"Your shell. This is your chance."

"I'm not in any shell."

"Cocoon, then."

She laughed. "Are you calling me a larva? Immature?"

They were in the garage. She had been straightening the paint cans, boxes and tools on the shelves against the rear wall. He persisted. Maybe she should take him up on it. He needed help, maybe she could help him. Would he let his stepmother into his confidence? Maybe not, but he might let a friend.

"Okay."

"Great!"

"I'll give it a whirl. I just hope I don't end up being scraped off the pavement."

They went outside to where the Harley leaned on its kickstand. Cheryl eyed it dubiously.

"Just remember to keep your feet planted on the foot-rests," he said. "Don't let them dangle. The tailpipe gets hot. You don't want to singe your ankle."

"Oh, wonderful."

"You won't, just keep your feet on the rests."

She put on her down jacket and dark glasses. Angela's helmet fit without adjusting the inside strap. She got on behind David.

"Hang on under your seat, or onto me. Whichever. Ready?"

"Don't go crazy, this isn't the turnpike."

The Harley turned over on the first kick. He roared it in neutral so loudly she thought she saw the front windows shake. The woman across the street came out carrying a watering can as an excuse to gawk. David waved to her. Cheryl grabbed hold under the seat, changed her mind and threw her arms around him.

"Hang on!"

Off they roared, cutting through the wind, leaning low around the corner into the straightaway and vaulting her heart into her throat. Instant exhilaration! A rocket launching! He hunched over so that she had to hold on around his stomach. He had no stomach; under his jacket he was lean and hard, the result of conscientiously regular work-outs with the barbell and weights under his bed. His coiled strength set her tingling. A panther sprang, its coat gleaming, muscles rippling. Howard wasn't like this. This was raw power penetrating her arms, her upper body absorbing it.

It was as if he and the Harley were a single entity and she was welded to it. The wind slammed her cheeks, her legs, her arms locked around him. Faster, faster, breaking free, escaping the cage of self, the ordinary and its limitations, the re-straints from a life of rigid discipline imposed by her aunt.

She gasped, she felt wild and wonderful. She tightened her grip on him, crushing her breasts against his back and angled her head, pressing her ear to his heart. She suddenly yearned to get inside him, into his warmth and strength, pull him around her. She caught herself, sucking a breath between her teeth.

He was slowing. *No! Keep on! Faster! On and on and on. To distant, unfamiliar places, to and through the horizon.* Only he slowed, the roaring in her ears softening, dying, as he pulled over to the curb.

"You can let go . . ."

She got off. Her cheeks tingled furiously. Was she blushing? Was it all from the wind?

"A block away like I promised."

The Harley idled. She felt as if she were slowly spiraling down to earth. He grinned. Did he know the effect it had had on her? He had to.

"So . . . ?"

"Wild."

"That's what they all say. Just what your soul needed, a blowing out. You like it, which means we'll have to do it again. Only next time not just putting along. Out on the highway where we can open her up. Say, why don't I pick you up when you get off work? Right here. Nobody'll see."

"No thanks. I've had enough for one day."

Why was she blushing? It was fantastic. Everything blown away by the wind made room for the most extraordinary im-pression: more than freedom, much more. Transfiguration! And it lingered gloriously. She wanted to dance in gratitude, instead she handed him the helmet. He resecured the straps and hung it on the handlebar, waved and took off, the motor roaring. She blinked once and he was out of sight around the corner.

She sighed and felt her cheeks. Still warm, still red. Maybe she should walk around the block before going to work.

Chapter Seven

Cheryl had broiled filet mignon for dinner. All three preferred their steak pink inside but the filets were medium. Carlos Montoya's flamenco guitar wafted soft music from the stereo in the living room. Dinner was later than usual. She had put the steaks on when Howard walked in the door at ten after eight.

"I took them out of the oven too late," she explained. "The timing has to be just right; you take them out, they keep broiling, that's when they turn pink. Take them out pink, they sit and turn medium."

"It's too complicated for me," said Howard. "Mine is perfect."

"Angela cooked steak three or four times while she was here and it always came out exactly the way she wanted it, remember? She was amazing. She never even had to cut into the meat to check. Now that's talent . . ."

"Mine is fine, too," said David.

Howard swallowed. "You're right, dear, she was some kind of cook. Oh, not that you're not . . ."

"Remember the time she sauteed filet mignon?" Cheryl continued. "Her sauce that night was out of this world."

"Are you putting on weight?" Howard asked David.

"Nine pounds so far. Of course I had nowhere to go but up."

Howard grinned. "That's your cooking, dear, so stop knocking it."

"Angela's cooking."

She was talking about Angela as if she'd just stepped out and was expected back momentarily. It had been almost two weeks since she left. Luckily for David, if luck could be attached to the situation, her departure coincided with an avalanche of schoolwork. Or was it possible he was glad that she left, even grateful? Farfetched, perhaps, but over the final two weeks, their life together had been very rocky. All the fighting must have been distracting for him. He was more relaxed, he rarely fidgeted. He smiled more, too, a nice smile.

"I've been thinking," he said, looking from one to the other. "With Angie gone, I should move out. Get a room in the city near the campus. It'd be cheap, not like an apartment."

Howard shook his head from first word to last. "Her leaving makes no difference. This is still your home, we're still your family, we should stay together."

"This *is* your home," said Cheryl.

She surprised herself. The day Angela left she couldn't wait to get him out of the house. Now she was prepared to argue that he stay.

Howard continued. "You left and we were out of touch for so long that when you finally did come home, we were strangers. But since then, especially since Angela left, I feel closer to you. I really look forward to our golf on Saturdays, to meals, sitting around chewing the fat. So do you, I can tell. You move out on us, we'll never get to see each other. And Cheryl needs someone around when I'm not here, don't you, dear?"

"I feel safer. And you're good company, David."

"It was just a thought . . ."

He offered to pay room and board. He was already bringing home more than his share of groceries. Howard wouldn't hear of it and pointedly changed the subject back to the meal.

"I don't care what you say, Cheryl, this steak is superb!"

"It's still overcooked."

"You miss her, don't you," said David.

"Yes."

"I'm sure she misses you."

Angela as focus of attention hung in the air. Howard re-filled Cheryl's wine glass.

"How about some wine, David?" she asked.

"A taste," said Howard. "It's burgundy. Great with steak."

"Why not?"

He got himself a glass, Howard poured for him. David raised his glass, eyed it.

"I don't remember who said it, but there's a quote about Noah. He was dining with his wife. He said, 'I don't care where the water goes if it doesn't get into the wine.'"

Howard laughed. Cheryl liked this. It was the way it should be. David was making the effort. The two of them were talking much more easily and spontaneously. No more fencing. She sensed that David was beginning to like her as well, picking up on how she felt about him.

For dessert she served freshly-baked apple pie. She had confidence in her baking, infinitely more than in her cooking. Talent like Angela's nearly awed her.

"Howard," she said, "I made a doctor's appointment for you today. It's time . . ."

"Annual physical," he explained to David. "I don't know why I bother, I'm in good shape." He patted his midriff. "No pot. I feel good, sleep good, exercise, drink in moderation. It's a waste of money, dear."

"This coming Tuesday. Four P.M. is the latest I could get. Oh, you won't be out of town?"

"I'll be here. Say, why not come into town and meet me at Garber's office? You'll be at school, David, how about we all make a night of it? Celebrate my clean bill of health. Try the burgundy, son."

He sipped. "Fruity . . . Tuesday sounds fine."

"Smooth as velvet, right?" Howard resumed eating. "You bake the best apple pie in the world, Cheryl. We could do with some cheddar cheese, though."

Dear Howard, she thought, watching him enjoying his pie. So dear, always trying to please her. When he had asked her out it had been a surprise; he was so much older than she. Nineteen years? That was nothing.

Cheryl had been on her own for several years then. Her great-aunt had died, leaving her income to an obscure charity and Cheryl had moved into a tiny apartment. She had been working at Clifton, Adams and Drury Industries since her return from New York and now considered herself enormously independent.

Her first real date with Howard had been enjoyable. She remembered feeling awkward, thinking nearly twenty years, nearly twenty years. . . . And she was worried people would take them for father and daughter. Only he didn't act "fatherly." Strait-laced, perhaps, as he often admitted himself, a bit of a fuddy-duddy, but not paternal. Most importantly, she was cherished from the outset of their relationship. A novel and wondrous feeling. Her contentment, her happiness were very important to him. He was a gentleman and consistent in temperament. She enjoyed listening to him.

That she was so much younger didn't appear to bother him, not even when they bumped into friends. Nobody commented on their relationship, at least not that she ever heard.

After they'd been dating for several months, thoughts of marriage arose, what it would be like. All the obvious advantages would be hers, beginning with faithfulness, stability, security, all valuable assets.

She fell in love with Howard Joyner as he did with her. At first he hesitated but when she accepted his proposal, he

---

couldn't tell her often enough. What he was, what he offered, she'd never found anywhere else.

David skipped his Spanish class on Monday. The course was a snap, earning the required credit would be no problem. Cheryl had a day off from the library. He was out in the driveway tinkering with the Harley most of the morning. Around half past eleven she left the house.

"I have to go into town for a couple of things, want to come along?"

"I should, I have to pick up my sports jacket and shirts at the dry cleaners. Give me a minute. I have to wash my hands and get my wallet."

It was getting on toward the end of September. There was a nip in the air at night but the days continued warm, pleasant. She waited outside for him. Looking down, she spotted a sprig of crabgrass and pulled it out for Howard. She wondered about his pending physical exam. He certainly looked and acted healthy. David pushed open the screen door.

"Shall we take the bike?"

"Let's walk."

He snickered. "You don't like the neighbors seeing you on it, do you?"

"I don't mind, it's nobody's business."

"It's not Mavis Delaney's, that's for sure. I'll make a biker out of you yet. One of these days we'll take her out on the turnpike, open her up. You did promise . . ."

"I did not. You suggested it. I didn't say a thing."

Downtown, they walked by Howard's barber shop, the blue-and-red striped sign slowly revolving, the three chairs sitting empty. Tony and Mario sat reading magazines. Across the street was the restaurant where she and Angela had had lunch the day Angela applied for the job at Alice Bowden's Dress Shop. Next door to the restaurant was the pharmacy.

"I have to stop at the drugstore."

He indicated the dry cleaners, three doors from the barber shop. "I'll pick up my cleaning and meet you out front."

At the counter an Asian girl about fourteen, in pigtails and a Holland Springs High School sweatshirt, waited on him. He wondered why she wasn't in school. He handed her both his receipts. She went straight to his tweed jacket on the revolving rack, laying it on the counter in its plastic wrapping. She checked his shirt receipt number against an array of pale green boxes shelved behind her. He could hear steam hissing behind the curtain at the rear. Someone laughed. Somebody else was jabbering angrily. He watched the clerk search and thought of Zhu Bocheng. She found the matching number.

"Four shirts."

"Right."

She added the total, he paid and walked outside. Cheryl waved as she started across the street. He had draped his jacket over his arm. As she approached, he opened the shirt box to check the number of shirts.

"All set?" she asked.

"All set. Wait, wait, what's this? There's blood on the collar of this one."

"You must have cut yourself shaving."

"I never noticed it. They obviously missed it. Don't they launder the whole shirt?"

"It didn't come out, it happens."

"Great, now it's ironed in, sealed by the heat. What a bunch of slobs . . ."

"Don't get upset."

"It'll never come out!"

"They'll get it out. Take it back in and show them."

She watched him through the window. He was scowling, too angry over a mistake so easily rectified. He exploded too often—she'd seen it with Angela half a dozen times. Had he been that way before Vietnam? She went inside. The clerk was still examining the stain. She looked helpless. David was making her nervous.

"How could this happen?" he demanded.

The girl held the shirt, turned from him, turned back.

"Miss . . . ? Miss . . . ? I'm talking to you."

"David, calm down."

"Practically brand new and it's ruined! Hey, where are you going?" The clerk retreated behind the curtain. He threw up his hands. He was seething. "How do you like this!"

"Shhhh . . ."

She reappeared, a man with her holding the shirt.

"Is blood, mister. You cut yourself shaving. I don't know how this happen it still there, but we fix, no problem."

David's eyes were huge. Cheryl watched as he shrank back, his hands came up, protecting himself. As he backed away, he nearly upset a potted ficus tree in the front window. He turned, jerked open the door and ran out.

"What the matter with him?"

"I'm sorry about this," said Cheryl. "Take care of the shirt. I'll pick it up later in the week."

"Wait, wait . . ."

The clerk handed her David's receipt. Outside, he was standing by the curb, sweating, trembling, the color drained from his face.

"It's all right, all settled," she said.

"I'm sorry. I apologize."

"What is the matter?"

"Nothing."

"He came through the curtain and it was like you'd seen a ghost."

"I did, Lieutenant Du, Shark Eyes. He captured me, brought me to the Sty. He was a devil, a sadist . . ."

"What did he do to you?"

"I see him in my nightmares as much as I see Woodrow. It's uncanny but that guy looked like Du's twin."

"But you've seen him before . . ."

"No, only her or the other girl."

"He's the owner. He took over the business about two years ago."

"That face . . ."

She got out a tissue. "Wipe your forehead. We have to stop at the supermarket and pick up a few things then we'll go straight home."

He stopped trembling. "No. I'm okay now. We're here, let me take you to lunch. We both have a day off, it doesn't happen that often, let's take advantage of it."

"If you like."

"I'm sorry I acted like an idiot. Sight of him just shocked me so . . ." He shook away the image.

"You're sure you're all right?"

"Let's go eat."

After lunch they went home to get the Harley and drove out to the park, about a mile east of town. He was still disturbed and embarrassed. They were preparing to pull into a parking space when a gleaming red sports car roared up behind them, horn blaring, swung around the Harley and cut them off, stealing the space. David battled to control the Harley.

"You idiot!" The driver jumped out and ran off waving a hand over his head dismissing them. "I could kill him . . . kill him!"

He looked as if he could.

"Please, it's nothing. People do it all the time."

"Not to me!" They found another place, a few spaces beyond. He cut the engine, she got off, he kicked down the stand. "Keep an eye out for him. If I see . . ."

"You'll do nothing. Forget him. I mean it, David. Are we going to walk around for the next two hours with you fuming?"

"No, but I still hope we bump into him."

"I hope so, too. It'll give you a chance to practice a little self-control."

He grunted. "The point is we both could have been hurt."

"We weren't. It's over."

Elementary school was over for the day. They watched mothers and nannies and teenaged baby-sitters helping children onto the merry-go-round. They got on. He was still annoyed. Over what had happened or the incident at the dry cleaner's? He had a hard time shaking off setbacks. The macho strain could be diminished, but never eliminated entirely. Then, too, maybe he hadn't progressed as far as she thought, in readjusting.

The park surrounded the merry-go-round. Vendors dispensed popcorn, ice cream and food from gleaming carts under red and white umbrellas. The mechanical band in the hub of the merry-go-round clanged, clattered and thumped. Cheryl's horse rose and descended. David stood beside her like a conscientious parent, gripping the brass pole.

"Grab the ring . . ."

She tried and missed twice. A shout went up; somebody behind her got it. The park whirled around them, the neatly-planted beds of fading dahlias and zinnias, the trees, the grass shining green, women and children and a few men. He stood holding on. She could feel his eyes following her up and down motion. She focused on his hand. It looked capable of pulling loose a chunk of the pole. She was tempted to run her fingertips along his index finger, just to touch and feel his warmth. His trigger finger that killed, and turned the pages of his Bible, and the collection of Christina Rossetti's poems.

Gradually, since Angela left, he was losing the fire and brimstone in his religion. Changing. He had tried wine, he no longer stiffened when his father slipped a swear word into the conversation. His toleration level appeared to be increasing. Angela's walking out had been a catalyst for change. He knew what he'd done to her, the little things that had accumulated and drove her away. He knew he was the cause, not her job problems, not the town or the people. He seemed to be shedding the Reverend Crowder facet of his personality that she had so disliked. Humanity was taking hold. Cheryl's sympathy for all he'd suffered was increasing. She liked him. They had a rapport.

On the way to the park on the Harley she had experienced the same tantalizing sensation that she'd felt the first time, her reason for not wanting to take it into town that morning. He was wrong. It wasn't the neighbors' disapproval or Mavis Delaney's that made her hesitate, it was she herself. She was afraid of liking it too much.

He brought his other hand up, holding onto the pole, absent-mindedly grinding it. He was very strong. He would put on more weight, fill out his upper body, upper arms. With that waist and those shoulders when summer came, he'd look beautiful in a T-shirt. Women would notice him.

The merry-go-round slowed, stopped, the music dying pathetically. They got off with most of the others. A small boy stood crying into his fist. He held an empty ice cream cone, a ball of vanilla at his feet. He probably hadn't even gotten to taste it.

"I saw what happened," said David. "Those two older kids over by the fountain ran by him. One grazed his elbow. Disaster."

"Here now," she said kneeling. "It's all right. My name's Cheryl, what's yours?"

She wiped his eyes with a tissue, he blew his nose on it.

"Those big guys stink!"

"Where's your mother?"

"Grandma. She's over there . . ."

He pointed to a woman sitting on a bench, a folded newspaper in her lap. She was asleep, her chins down on her bosom, glasses hanging from slender chains glinting in the sun, her left hand clutching the wooden handles of a knitting bag. Cheryl looked around. David had walked off. She spotted him at an ice cream cart. He came back with a vanilla cone, handing it to the boy. The sun shone on his freckled face. He blurted out thanks and ran toward his grandmother.

"That was sweet."

"Ounce of prevention. He looked like he was about to pick up the gob he dropped."

They walked around until midafternoon. They talked, they people watched. She had a wonderful time.

Two eight-inch sterling silver fishhooks supported Dr. Mills Garber's desk lamp. He sat at his desk looking, as usual, aggressively tanned and fit. One wall displayed color photographs of him holding his fishing pole beside ten and twelve-foot marlin, tarpon and swordfish. On his desk facing Cheryl was a photo of his wife and three uncontrollably blond sons. His wife stood behind them squinting into the sun. Her blondness was by choice, as the dark roots flanking her part confirmed. The other walls were devoted to Dr. Garber. Among each framed flurry of Latin could be seen the name of a college, his name and a date, milestones in his journey to his various degrees.

"Iris is finishing up Howard's EKG."

"Everything okay?"

"We have to wait for his blood work to come back. He looks and feels good. One thing . . ." His chair squeaked as he turned slightly and began tapping the blotter with his pen. The four shoulder buttons of his tunic gleamed in the light of the fishhook lamp. "His blood pressure is quite elevated, one sixty-two over one sixteen. Iris took it three times to be absolutely sure."

"That's very high. What can you do?"

"What can *he* do. Weight can raise it but he's not overweight. He doesn't drink too much. What he really needs is exercise."

"He plays golf."

Garber snickered. "Golf is excellent exercise for the cart. I mean sweating, puffing." He got out a pamphlet. "Sit-ups, leg-ups, push-ups, running in place, the old standbys. Twenty to thirty minutes every other day. He doesn't need six thousand dollars worth of equipment. Make him read that, crack the whip. It could also be stress-related. How's everything at Great Lakes Re?"

"Fine, he doesn't complain. There's always pressure, long hours."

"He could be overdoing it."

"He has always loved his work."

"He needs to play, a hobby. Horseback riding is good, rock climbing, racket ball . . ."

"Stamp collecting."

"Mr. Sedentary."

"He does stand, mostly at airports."

"Harriet, my wife, is into water skiing. She loves it. Well, anything'll do for Howard, anything to get him out of himself, push business out of his mind for a few hours. His numbers really should come down." He scribbled a prescription. "This'll help, but it's no cure. I want him back in seven days to check his pressure. By then his blood work'll be back, too. Is he active around the house? Is he Mr. Fix-it or does he just change light bulbs?"

"I change the light bulbs."

"He should exercise but his hobby doesn't necessarily have to be physical."

"I can guarantee it won't be."

"You look in good shape, what do you do?"

"I walk everywhere. I volunteer at the library, lots of bending, squatting, stretching."

"It shows. So here we are, get Howard into something. It's important, Cheryl, ounce of prevention and all that . . ."

"I'll do my best."

The door opened. The nurse, squinting astigmatically behind thick lenses, stood behind Howard as he put on his jacket. He came in grinning.

"I've got the heart of a sixteen-year-old. Tell 'em, Iris. Tell this guy. And don't worry about my blood pressure. I'm going off the sauce. Oh, maybe one martini a night. All set, Cheryl? Let's get a move on, we've got to meet Dave."

"How is Dave?" Garber asked. "Getting back into the swing of things?"

"He's great, couldn't be better. He's going to OSU, studying religion."

"Religion?"

Howard laughed. "Everybody reacts to that the same way. He wants to teach it."

"Good for him. Give him my best, tell him welcome home. Tell him if he wants to talk, give us a jingle."

They went out. Offices were emptying for the day, the elevators were packed and moving slowly. They stood and waited, eyes fixed on the floor indicator lights. Letters shot by heading down the mail chute.

"Where does Mills get that stuff?" Howard asked. "What makes him think David wants to talk to him? Does he think David's screwed up? Damn, that elevator went right by, did you see? Cheryl, don't worry, I've never felt better and that's the God's honest truth. I'll get my blood pressure down. One martini limit, exercise, a hobby . . ."

"A lot of veterans coming home are having psychological problems, dear. I've been reading and watching a lot about the war lately. It's nothing like World War II."

"Isn't that obvious?"

"I'm talking about the effect it has on those involved. In World War II, nobody was confused about the objective. It was us against the bad guys to save the world. People were proud to take part, everybody pitched in, patriotism flourished. This war's different."

"Cheryl, we're over there to save the country from the Communists, save all of southeast Asia. What's confusing about that?"

"Some people think all we're doing is pulling France's chestnuts out of the fire. Our interests aren't at stake, at least not directly. It's not like when Japan attacked Pearl Harbor and the Axis overran Europe. As far as David's concerned personally, maybe he never questioned what we're doing there, but I can't help suspecting he became disillusioned. He's sure brought home a lot of baggage."

"Look at that, now neither elevator's moving. He has but he's shaking it off. Gradually. He doesn't need Mills Garber messing about inside his head."

"I think it was nice of him to offer to talk. He's probably

talked to a few veterans."

"So you think Dave is screwed up."

"I don't think he's readjusted completely yet. You don't either, you said so."

"He's not screwed up. Not like some. I will admit this wanting to study and teach religion is strange, especially for somebody whose mother and I had to practically drag to Sunday School."

"It may be that religion is a refuge for him."

"Now? With it all behind him?"

"But it's not all behind him. He still has nightmares. I'm sure he relives his time in that prison camp. And the fighting, the killing, suffering. You can't throw a switch and blot it all out."

"What he should do is talk about it, spill his guts, purge himself of it. Oh no, he'd rather hold it all in. You think I should tell him about Mills's offer to talk? Maybe not, maybe he'll think we talked about him behind his back." He sighed. "I wish to hell I could do something."

"You're getting closer to him, that helps."

"Not much. You, you're doing fine with him. He was cool toward you starting out but he's really changed since Angela left. You should make him your number one rehabilitation project."

"*He's* working on that. All I can do is be a friend. Try and help without interfering."

"What he needs is a job. Throw himself into it. That'll get rid of his 'baggage' quicker than anything. Here's the elevator, at last."

Chapter Eight

"The refractor's eighty millimeters, that's three-point-one inches. Right angled eyepiece attachment. It makes for a more comfortable viewing position at all angles of the telescope. And look here, this is what they call a dewcap. It extends out front of the objective lens. The guy at the store says that everybody prefers the refractory type telescope. It gives the best possible definition. Reflector telescopes don't come close. I don't want to bore you two, but I'm really getting into this."

"Where will you put it?" David asked.

"Up in the attic. We've got three windows close to the roof. I can move it around. No trees in the way, no wires, nothing."

He'd set up his new telescope in the living room and called them in.

"And this is it. Initial expense and nothing more, not like a camera. Though I will buy a couple of books." He got a note out of his pocket. "The salesman gave me these four names. I can pick the books up in San Francisco. Look at me, you two, I'm really excited. Like a kid with a new toy. Me, an astronomer, at least a stargazer, right?"

"It's a wonderful idea," agreed Cheryl.

"By the way, one of you'll have to drive me to the airport." Howard checked his watch. "I'm catching an eight-fifty plane."

"We'll both take you," said David. "What time is it now?"

"You're wearing your new watch, look at it."

"Six-thirty," said Cheryl.

"Have I time to set this up in the attic before dinner?"

"Go to it."

"Let me help you," said David. Howard had picked up the assembled telescope and started up the stairs. David lowered his voice. "My father, the observer of the infinite."

"Don't make fun of him, I think it's a fine idea. Help him, dinner'll be ready in twenty minutes."

They saw Howard off at the airport for a three-day trip.

"Let's not go home right away," said David.

"Where do you want to go?"

"The amusement park. It closes for the season the first of October. I'd like to see it, see if it's changed any since high school. A bunch of us used to go at least once a week."

The amusement park glared and twinkled with lights, people wandered about eating, men and women called behind counters to get their attention, hawking games of chance and skill, promising prizes for knocking down pyramids of six metal bottles or fur-fringed monkeys, for guessing the right number on a spinning wheel, for a winning poker hand, and other tests of skill, accuracy and luck. They had just finished a rambunctious test of both their driving skills in bumper cars. He started talking about Angela. He seemed to want to purge her from his system. Talking helped.

"She loved me, she loved me for the dangers I had passed. And I loved her that she did pity them."

"Poetic. Original?"

"Original Shakespeare. Othello speaking to the Duke of Venice about Desdemona. But it says it all about Angie and me. She deserves credit, Cheryl, whether she planned it or not, she woke me up, opened my eyes to a lot of things wrong with me. Too late for our marriage, though. I'm not the same person I was when I came back, am I?"

"You're very different. I didn't like that David. I could list the things I disliked, but you know them. You didn't like me back then, either."

"I couldn't stand you. There weren't enough things to dislike, I had to look for more. Angie at least started straightening me out. Let's not talk about back then . . ."

They were passing a shooting gallery. Shots whacked and pinged as they struck targets, making bells ring. Behind the proprietor, Ping-Pong balls danced on jets of water, wooden ducks glided in and out of view, moving targets revolved; under a fatigue cap, an ancient face scowled.

"Here you go, champ," the man behind the counter called, offering David a rifle. The tattoos on his arms were faded with age, he wore a two-inch brass ring in one ear, his bald head gleamed in the glaring light. "Let's see your eagle eye. Knock down five ducks, win a stuffed panda for the missus."

"Try it," urged Cheryl. "I bet you'll knock down every one."

She took hold of his arm starting toward the counter. At one end a high school kid was showing off for his date. At the other stood three men in Air Force uniforms; a fourth wore a flight jacket with an intricately designed dragon sewn on the back, under it, "Saigon," with each letter inscribed in flames. The four men stared at David.

"I'd rather not, Cheryl."

"Come on, champ," persisted the proprietor. "Be a sport, show us how good you are."

"Show us," called one of the airmen.

The two that were shooting had put down their guns. They'd been drinking and one held a bottle of whiskey. They frowned at David.

"What's the matter, champ, you chicken?" one taunted.

"You a damn peacenik?"

"Hey, Joe, chrissakes, leave the guy alone . . ."

"I asked you a question, fella."

"Let's go, Cheryl. No guns."

"No guns," jeered the dragon jacket. "You hear him? He's a peacenik."

"Leave him alone, boys," said the proprietor.

People passing had stopped to watch.

"Shut-up, old man. Come on, peacenik, let's see your shooting eye. Come here, I'll show you how to hold the damn thing . . ."

"Come on," murmured Cheryl.

David hesitated, debating. They started walking away.

"That's it, Mama, take him away. He might hurt himself!"

"Take him home, tuck him in bed," called dragon jacket.

They burst into laughter. Some in the crowd joined them. David stopped and turned around. Cheryl pulled him along.

"They're drunk . . ."

"Jerks."

"I'm thirsty, let's get a soda."

"I couldn't do it. All those rifles lined up on the counter were like snakes. I couldn't even touch one, let alone pick it up. Never again. I swore before I got away no matter what happened I'd never pull another trigger."

"Forget about it. Are you all right?"

He stopped, freeing his arm from her hold. "Why do you always ask if I'm all right? What am I, your patient?"

"Don't talk to me like that, I'm concerned, that's all."

"About what? I'm doing the best I can. Can't you see that? Can't you see I'm trying?"

"Of course you are."

"Don't patronize me!"

"I'm not. Let's just drop it. What do you want to do?"

They hung around awhile longer, giving him time to simmer down. It was almost eleven when they walked into the house. He plumped down in a chair.

"Would you do me a favor?" he asked.

"What?"

"Play something."

"Now?"

"Please. 'Prelude in D flat.' "

She sat and ran her fingers up and down the scale then flexed and kneaded them. She played. It was a familiar choice, one they both liked. He could have hummed along. Instead, he sat quietly, not taking his eyes off her. The melody emerged liltingly. A few bars into it she looked up and caught his eyes. From that point on she could not take her eyes from his. On she played, each of them holding the other. The *Prelude* ran a little over five minutes. She finished and sat a moment. Then she closed the piano and stood.

"Beautiful," he said.

"Bedtime."

He declined her offer of a cup of tea even when she insisted, touting it as better than milk for inducing sleep. She made tea for herself, letting him have the bathroom first. She brought a second cup upstairs. A rod of light showed under his door. He was studying. She set a hand against the door.

Something was happening. Not "something"—she knew what it was. They had both done an about face since Angela left. Starting from scratch, the mutual dislike, the mistrust, the coolness had been put aside. When Angela left, he reached out for help, reached toward his stepmother, touching a maternal chord. Since that afternoon sympathy had evolved into fondness.

Was there cause for worry? Their relationship mustn't get out of hand. It was her job to maintain control, not leave it up to him. No woman in her right mind entrusted the man with the reins of a "just good friends" relationship.

From now on they mustn't touch each other. When he was gripping the pole on the merry-go-round she'd been tempted to set her hand against his. She hadn't done so, thank heavens. It would have sent the wrong signal. No touching, resist the urge to squeeze his hand, lay her hand on his arm, even pat him on the back in encouragement. And don't be warm. How could she control that? If you weren't warm toward someone you were cold, at best indifferent. He didn't deserve either.

She must avoid his eyes. No more staring like during the *Prelude*. And be on her guard. Both must keep their guards up. If necessary, sit down and discuss it before the situation got out of hand. No, not possible.

Were the same concerns troubling him? That could be. She took her hand down from the door, stepping back, whispering.

"Good night, David."

She was in the driveway washing the car when he came down to breakfast. Her feet were bare, her hair pinned up under a kerchief. He had told her the night before that he had an eleven o'clock in biology. They greeted each other. The hose snaked away from the faucet at the front of the house to the nozzle dribbling on the pavement. She was soaping the driver's door.

"Let me help . . ."

"You've got a class."

"I've got hours."

"What about breakfast?"

"I just had coffee."

He retrieved the hose and tried to adjust the nozzle. A fine spray squirted. He tried to loosen the nozzle further but it stuck. When he finally got it to turn, the water shot forth so powerfully he lost his hold. It whipped out of control, drenching Cheryl. She yelled. A passing driver grinned and honked comment.

"You did that on purpose!"

"I did not, it got away from me . . ."

"Liar!"

She was soaking. She pulled off her kerchief, flinging it to the ground. She shook the water off her hands, running them down her front and glared. Her dress stuck to her and she tried to pick the material away but it clung soggily, outlining every curve of her body. Her eyes narrowed. She lunged for the nozzle, wresting it from him, turning it on him, shouting.

His sweatshirt and slacks soaked, he stood dripping. "Give me that!"

She kept spraying him, retreating, evading his reach. She tangled her feet in a loop of the hose and he pulled on it, tripping her with the loop.

"Gotcha!"

She lay helplessly laughing, her dress pulled up above her knees. The woman across the street gawked at them from her front window. David aimed the hose at her but the spray barely reached the middle of the street, and she retreated. Cheryl took advantage of the distraction, jumped to her feet and ran to the faucet. She turned it off, coming back slowly, wringing out the hem of her dress. She felt icy all over.

"You rat . . . now I've got to take another shower!"

"You don't need one, you look fine." He laughed. "Just run a comb through your hair. Tell Mavis a pipe burst." He sobered. Almost like a reflex, he murmured, "God, you're beaut . . ."

"Do you mind not gaping at me? Look what you've done. The hood and front were practically dry. Look, look . . ."

"I'll do the whole car."

"Never mind, just go. Wait. . . ." Nozzle in hand, she ran back to the faucet and turned on the water.

He backed away warily. "What are you doing?"

"Your Harley's filthy."

"No you don't! Cheryl . . . Cheryl!"

Into the garage she ran and began spraying the Harley. He snatched the hose from behind her and pulled it away. The water snaked across the floor as he bent to retrieve the nozzle.

"Are you nuts? It'll ruin it!" He shut the water off at the nozzle.

"It won't. Rain doesn't hurt it, why should a little water? Wheel it outside, throw some oil on it, it'll be fine. At least it's clean for a change. Let's go for a ride. Twice around the block'll dry it off. Dry us, too!"

"What's come over you?"

"You started it." She laughed and started for the door. "First one upstairs gets the shower!"

"What about the car?"

"First oil the Harley. And not too much soap on the car."

He was shivering as he dried the spark plugs and other parts. The neighbor across the street reappeared in her window for another look. He paused in drying the Harley. Listening intently, he could hear the sound of the shower through the open upstairs window, and Cheryl singing happily.

Chapter Nine

Cheryl went to work at nine o'clock when the library opened the next morning, coming home in the middle of the afternoon. Walking home, she thought about their actions in the driveway and what it must have looked like to anyone watching. It was harmless, nevertheless, drawing a line between innocent fun and what was "over the line" wasn't easy.

In the kitchen she found a note magneted to the refrigerator, a single word: "table." Years ago somebody had built a picnic table large enough to seat four, setting it up in the woods at the end of Warren Avenue. It was available to anybody in the neighborhood who wanted to use it. Time and weather had abused it, names and initials, gouges and crude drawings distressed the surface. Still it endured and served, hosting picnics and card games and supporting forearms of people who just came to sit and settle the weightier problems of the world.

Occasionally David took advantage of the peaceful surroundings and the privacy to study at the table. Starting at the end of the street was a path through black and white oaks, hickories, ashes and beeches. The glade, with the table set up in the center of it, was roughly twenty feet in diameter. She came upon him bent over a book, highlighting passages with a yellow marker. He didn't hear her approach.

"David . . ."

He started and grinned, "You made it. Good, good . . ."

A horned lark showed its black and yellow face from a branch stretching above their heads. It flicked its tail, assessed them and flew off, its ti-ti song trailing after it in a series of tinkling notes.

"Homework?"

"Just killing time waiting for you. Breaking down Moses and Elijah for an oral this Thursday." He closed the book. It lay at an angle. *Personalities of the Old Testament.* "I wanted to talk away from the house, the phone, distractions."

He seemed self-conscious, nervous about what he was planning to say.

"Talk about what?"

"Me. What else? In case it's escaped your notice, I'm unique. I've a talent for collecting guilt."

"If you mean Angela . . ."

"I don't. Cheryl, there's something I want to tell you, something I never told her and I can't tell Pop. Maybe you'll understand, maybe not."

He paused. "You remember Clive Holbrook."

"Your friend who was killed."

"*I* killed him."

"No."

"Oh, I didn't pull the trigger. That's not what killed him. We were going over the fence. I was on the outside ladder, he was inside. They shot him in the shoulder, so that he couldn't grab hold with his right hand. I could have helped him over." He stared down at the table. He began turning the closed book in a circle. Carved initials appeared and vanished. "He wasn't badly hurt. Painfully, but not badly. He just couldn't lift that arm."

He looked up, the suffering she hadn't seen in weeks had returned. "I never told Angie, I was just ashamed . . ."

The lark came back. It pecked about on the ground nearby. He looked through it.

"I could have helped him but I didn't. I ignored his pleading and saved myself. I left him hanging on the fence, a target. I relive it again and again in my nightmares. I see his face, his eyes, his helplessness. I hear him calling after me. I deserted him, to save myself."

"That's ridiculous. You're right about one thing, though, you really have dedicated yourself to collecting guilt. You've elevated it to an art form."

"I abandoned him. His eyes shouted it. They didn't accuse, there was no fear in them, only shock: that I, his friend, would leave him hanging. I didn't panic, I can't use that for an excuse. I just flashed ahead and decided in a split-second that even if I got him over and down safely he was in such bad shape he'd never make it."

"Aren't you overlooking something? Isn't it a normal reaction to want to save yourself? Instinctive?"

"Is it normal to consciously and deliberately sacrifice somebody else to save yourself? Not just anybody but the one who made escape possible? I don't think so, and that's not all."

"What else is there?"

"The night I was captured seventeen men died."

"Killed by the enemy."

"By me."

"Nonsense . . ."

"True. Indisputable fact. I led all twenty of us into a trap. Seventeen men were mowed down, two got away, I was captured."

"How could you possibly know it was a trap?"

"I'd been out at least sixty times on patrol. You're supposed to learn from experience, right? Not me, I might as well have marched them in and massacred them myself."

"You're very good. Exceptional. However convoluted, however farfetched, you fit everything logically in place so you can assume the blame. You don't collect guilt, you hunt it down. What's next, did you personally start the war?"

"I'm serious."

She rose, setting her palms, heels toward the edge of the table and leaned over.

"So am I and I say bull."

"You just don't understand. You weren't there the night they slaughtered us."

" 'They' did? Or you? If you want my opinion, and you wouldn't have left the note if you didn't, I think the night of the ambush preyed on your mind all the way to the prison camp and all the time you were there. But at that stage it was limited to regret. It wasn't until Clive was killed that you assumed the guilt for what happened at the clearing, for every death where you were in charge."

"Congratulations, doctor. So now we have a psychoanalyst in the family."

"You started this. I'm curious, how much guilt do you have to take on before it's enough, before you're satisfied?"

"You think I'm a masochist."

"No. I think you make a sham of conscientiousness, carry it beyond the bounds of common sense."

Covering himself with guilt led him to religion, to purging himself. It was no refuge, it was a means of expiating his "sin." His Christianity teacher in Cambodia gave him the last push. That was it. She was tempted to tell him. He was telling her about Ngo and the other traitor, and how easy it had been to deduce their roles in the ambush.

"I trusted them."

"Hardly, you just didn't suspect them. Why should you? Who would?"

"This is not good. I thought talking about it would release the pressure."

"Blame me, I'm not saying what you want to hear. I'm supposed to agree . . ."

"I don't recall asking you to."

"You want me to. I can't. You've got it all wrong. There's not a grain of logic or truth in any of it. Don't tell me you had to be there. Does a judge have to be standing by when a crime is committed?"

She glanced at her watch.

"You want to go," he said. "I'll come . . ."

"I'm sorry I'm no help. I don't see how anybody can help you. It's your problem. It's up to your reasonable, unemotional self to deal with it. It might help if you got rid of the sackcloth and ashes."

"Aren't you being a little harsh?"

"Possibly. But not nearly as harsh as you're being on yourself. You're trying to wash blood off your hands that's not even there."

They walked home in silence to find the mail had been delivered. There was a letter from a New York law firm for David. Angela was filing for divorce. He was informed that papers would be arriving soon and if he agreed to the terms of the divorce, all he need do would be to sign and return them.

Chapter Ten

Dinner was over. David was helping Cheryl with the dishes when Howard asked her to come up to the attic. They made their way to the telescope across the planks set on the joists between beds of pink insulation. The front window looked out to the southeast. He opened it and positioned the telescope so that the tube protruded.

"Are you remembering to take your blood pressure pill?"

"Sure, sure, sure. This is fabulous, wait'll you see." He squinted into the eyepiece and adjusted the telescope. "Take a look . . ."

The moon looked blurred and unimpressive to the naked eye. Through the telescope the change was surprising.

"It looks stuccoed and the color is so clear. Vivid."

"Isn't that remarkable? That's almost dead center. Look left about ten o'clock. See that depression with the scalloped edge on the upper right? That's Mare Nectaris. The scallops are a line of craters: Theophilus, Catherina and Cyrillus. How big do you think? Sixty miles across. How about that?"

She straightened. "I like the different shades of blue and gray."

"That's caused by light pollution. We're too close to Columbus, the skies don't get truly dark. You have to be at least sixty miles from the nearest city of a million or more population, and greater Columbus is over a million. The best viewing point is pitch-black mountain tops or desert parks. The skies are unpolluted, magnificent. Mills Garber did me a favor, I love this!"

"What else have you seen?"

"Nothing, yet. I've been concentrating on the moon. Cheryl . . ."

"Yes?"

"Remember when I proposed and you accepted, I promised you the moon? It took awhile but here you are." He kissed her.

She squeezed him playfully. "Thank you, dear, it's something I've always wanted."

"That reminds me, somebody's birthday's coming up. Anything special you want?"

"Surprise me."

"You bet I will." He turned and looked through the eyepiece. "Dave say anything to you lately about school?"

"No, why?"

"We talked on the way home from the airport. He's not happy with OSU. He still resents having to take courses that have nothing to do with religion. He thinks the place is too big, a factory, too impersonal. Some of his classes have more than a hundred students. The professors don't even know students' names." He looked toward her, his gray eyes twinkling. "I honestly think he's beginning to sour on the whole idea."

"He said that?"

"Implied it. Don't be surprised if he quits cold."

"If he does he still doesn't want the job."

"Did he say that?"

"No . . ."

"There you are. Watch, I predict he'll drop out within a month. He's impulsive, it'll happen fast."

"Don't get your hopes up. He may quit, but not to work at Great Lakes."

"I don't agree, he could change his mind completely. He did once, he could change right back. I see Angela wants her divorce. Were you there when he read the lawyer's letter? Did he looked shocked?"

"Howard, he's been expecting it."

"You think he's gotten her out of his system."

"I think so."

"Me, too. Now if we can only get him to change his mind about the job, he'll be set for life."

"Howard, if you were an insect, you'd be a tick. You never let go."

"Whoa, we're talking about his future."

"Fine, just don't talk about it to him. Now, if you'll excuse me, I have to attend to the highlight of my day, turning on the dishwasher."

She lay abed that night thinking about what Howard had said. He'd implied that David was on the verge of dropping out, even allowing for Howard's tendency to overstate. Still David hadn't said one word to her. It didn't make sense. Why would he bare his soul at the picnic table and keep secret something not nearly as confidential?

He had to know Howard would tell her, so what game was he playing? Why not tell her himself? If he dropped out, he'd transfer, which meant he'd be moving out. He *would* transfer, not take the job with Great Lakes, no matter how much optimism Howard generated. The possibility of David leaving was disturbing. They'd become friends.

Should she talk to him about it? No. In confiding in Howard, David knew it would get back to her. That had to be his intention.

Chapter Eleven

Howard was home for only three days before leaving again, this time to Dallas.

"It may drag out to four days. I'm sorry, Cheryl, I hate missing your birthday."

They were getting out of the car in the short term parking lot. It had rained heavily, reducing the area to a quagmire.

"You and Dave'll just have to celebrate without me. I wish I could wriggle out of this, at least postpone it, but . . ."

"It's okay, dear, it's not as if my birthday was a national holiday. Take care of yourself. Got your pills?" He tapped his carry-on. The wind whipped the panels of his topcoat. "I worry, Howard, your blood pressure's not improving very fast."

"You heard Mills, we've got to be patient."

Inside, she waited as usual until they announced the seating for his flight. The loudspeaker blared scratchily. He kissed her.

"Happy birthday, dear. Dave is holding my gift, I hope you like it."

"I'll love it."

"Take care of him, Cheryl. I worry, he seems at loose ends lately. You've been a good friend when he really needed one. That helps. I'll phone you tomorrow, seven on the dot."

She grinned. "When the phone rings I'll make sure the clocks are right."

He kissed her and got into line, waving before he passed out of sight. She picked her way between puddles to the car and headed home preoccupied with thoughts of David. He *was* at loose ends. That morning he had admitted to her that

118

he was having second thoughts about OSU. Had he rushed to sign up to avoid further clashing with Howard over the job? She wished he'd change his mind and take it, at least give it a try. He might be pleasantly surprised, and he'd stay in the area. Howard and he would eventually grow closer. That would be ideal but it was also unrealistic. She doubted they would ever be any closer than they were now.

She turned into the approach road to the highway and waited at the stop sign for her chance to slip into the flow of traffic. No. He'd leave, dropping out of both their lives. She gunned the car, edging onto the highway.

A feeling of unease gripped her. She didn't want him to leave. Out of the question. She'd talk to him. As soon as she got home today. Maybe he could make changes at school, re-arrange classes, drop a course, substitute something else. If he knew how much both she and Howard wanted him to stay, maybe he could make allowances. There was even the possibility that another school more suitable to his needs was close by. He wouldn't have to leave then. No need.

On second thought, maybe she shouldn't say anything. He might resent her interfering.

"What a mess . . ."

That night David brought home Chinese food. She opened a bottle of Chablis. They ate in the kitchen, the cat watching them divide the chicken fried rice and share the shrimp and orange beef.

"What time do you go in tomorrow?" he asked.

"Noon, why?"

"It's your birthday, you should take the day off."

"I can't. A couple of the girls are away, we're short-handed."

"There's a Manet exhibit at the art museum in Columbus.

119

I like the Impressionists, I was thinking of catching it before it leaves. The museum opens at ten. My first class isn't till twelve-thirty. You could drive in, meet me at the door, we could stay till eleven-thirty. You'd be back in plenty of time for work . . ."

"I'd like that."

"And tomorrow night I'll take you to a birthday dinner."

"That's sweet of you, David, but you don't have to."

"I do. Pop would if he were here. I'll just be pinch-hitting for him. We'll have a night on the town. Then come home and have your party."

"It sounds like you're fomenting a full-scale celebration. Please don't . . ."

He leered. "What's your fortune?"

"You first."

He broke the cookie and read the slip. "Love, fire and coughing cannot be hidden."

"Brilliant. What's mine? 'On your guard, change will shortly come into your life'." She laughed. "Sure, somebody'll show up at the front door begging me to play Carnegie Hall."

Few people were waiting for the doors to open at the art museum. The Manet exhibit was comprised of thirty-one paintings and nearly twice that number of pen and ink sketches. Neither had ever seen a collection of Manet's work. Cheryl had always thought his nudes much more sensual than those of his contemporaries. She admired the simplicity of his style. He respected the female body and glorified it, he didn't show off, he wasn't vulgar.

She particularly liked *Olympia*, the way he rendered two narrow pink lines for the lips and reduced the eyes to a few black strokes. The program suggested that you view the painting up close then step back. When they did so, each object—the servant's bouquet, Olympia's slipper, her bracelet, the slender black ribbon around her neck, which set off so starkly the vivid whiteness of her flesh—fell into proper place.

Now they stood before *Luncheon on the Grass.* The nude sat in profile with two well-dressed men in a sylvan setting. Her right knee was upraised, her right arm flexed, her elbow against her knee. Her arm concealed the top of her breast, she held her fingers loosely against her chin.

"Her flesh is so vibrant," she whispered. "Even more so than Olympia."

"So warm and creamy. The contrast with their dark clothes makes it almost pulse. You know what this is? It's us three picnicking. And you forgot something."

She grinned. "The mayonnaise."

"She is beautiful . . ."

He was standing behind her and to her left. He set his hand on her shoulder. She felt warmth and tingled. The nude glowed; if the man sitting closest to her were to reach out and touch her he'd *feel* it.

"It's like the light is making love to her," he murmured. "The way it dazzles and skims and slips along, caressing her body."

His voice had taken on a huskiness in an effort to keep from being overheard. "Look at that face," he went on, "the way she's only half-listening to the man across from her. She's so detached, free, she doesn't even realize she's naked."

"No. She knows. And she's proud of her body. Reveling in it. If the artist covered any part of her, it would ruin the whole effect."

"He should have called it *Freedom.*"

"Freedom every woman fantasizes about."

Once more he commented on the model's flesh, how the natural light made it look luminous, like velvet flowing around her shoulder, her breast, her thigh. He whispered close to her ear. She felt his warm breath. She stared at the nude and the man sitting closest to her. Both seemed to be staring at an unseen individual staring at them. The man's expression was almost disdainful. At what, the observer's failure to understand, to appreciate her beauty and boldness? Cheryl envied her, there was nothing indecent in her nakedness. She was defying convention not to shock but to celebrate her body. Manet knew what he wanted to project, and he had succeeded.

She felt David's eyes on her. She turned, he turned away, but in that instant she saw something in his eyes. Longing? Desire? Not possible. He said nothing, he took her arm, they moved on to the next painting. She stood a little further from him as they studied it.

Cheryl came home from the library a few minutes after six to the sight of the piano strewn with red roses.

"David . . . !"

He emerged grinning from the kitchen, a Coke in hand.

"Happy birthday again. Want a Coke?"

"No thanks. They're beautiful! I haven't gotten flowers in ages. Howard is candy, not flowers."

"I shouldn't have left them out of water so long. They look tired. How long do roses last?"

"These'll last and last. Let's put them in water."

He filled her biggest Waterford vase.

"I'll make a reservation at Mezzaluna for eight, okay?"

"Fine, I love their *zuppa di clams*."

"It's your birthday, tonight is lobster *fra diavolo* and champagne."

Howard called from Dallas at seven. At seven-thirty they backed the car out and headed for the city. The interior of the Mezzaluna Restaurant suggested a grotto on the Isle of Capri: cave walls, torches in scones dispelling the pervading gloom and a stone ceiling pocked with hollows.

They were enjoying their dessert when four waiters descended on them with a cake and one lonely candle. They harmonized "Happy Birthday to You." It was conspicuous and corny but Cheryl was delighted. A nine-piece orchestra played for dancing. David surprised her. Howard was a good dancer, too, although he had a habit of humming the tunes he knew.

She was feeling a little tired by the time David led her onto the floor. Dancing revived her. He held her close for "When Joanna Loves Me." She liked it, recalling something like the same feeling when she sat close to him on the Harley the first time. His cheek against hers set her glowing. His warmth, radiating from his smile, seemed to enter her at every place they touched. As the band segued from one ballad to the next, dancing gave way to floating, as easily, as effortlessly as two silky milkweed parachutes propelled by the sun in motionless air. He no longer held her. He became an extension of her. They were one.

It was very late when she noticed they were the last couple on the floor. The musicians stopped playing and packed up their instruments, shattering the dreamy mood with yawning and laughter. The waiter glided toward them with the bill on a tray.

It was after one-thirty when they walked in the door. Adrenaline charged her, she felt as if she could dance all night, sleep was the last thing she needed. She felt glorious, she couldn't recall ever feeling quite like this, like a bride awakening the next morning. She stretched and whirled, dancing by herself. He sat her on the sofa.

"Presents. Pop's first. I'm afraid he forgot your card . . ."

"No he didn't. He doesn't believe in cards. He calls them printing press sentiment with the price on the back."

He gave her an envelope. "From him with love." Enclosed was a note. " 'To my beautiful wife on her birthday. Many happy returns and all that. I love you, Cheryl, desperately and forever'."

"I love you, Howard, 'desperately and forever'."

His present was a gift certificate from Alice Bowden's Dress Shop for five hundred dollars.

"Thank you, my darling."

"Five hundred . . ." murmured David. "Why does what I'm about to give you suddenly seem like a birdhouse I made myself?"

"Stop it."

She opened his handwritten card.

" 'Happy birthday to my best friend'."

She kissed him on the cheek and unwrapped his gift. It was a box about eight inches square. When she removed the lid she gasped. Inside was a replica of her piano.

"It's beautiful . . ."

"Beauty is as beauty does. It's a music box. I think it's already wound. Just raise the top."

It played the first eight bars of the "Prelude in D flat." It repeated the passage before winding down.

"I love it, David."

She wound it. It played, sprightly through the first rendition, somewhat forlornly near the end of the second. It touched her. Gloriously. It was so David.

"Oh geez . . ."

"What?"

"Don't you know you're not allowed to cry on your birthday?"

"They're happy tears."

She set the music box on the piano and put her arms around him. "I love it. I love you for thinking of it. But of course *you* would . . ." She kissed him. A friendly kiss, appreciation.

An hour later she went up to bed leaving him studying at the kitchen table. She undressed and sat at her vanity in her peignoir. She was still charged, she could still hear the music, still feel his arms around her. It was a strange feeling that had hold of her, both anxious and gratifying, a little frightening. They had touched and touched all evening. She couldn't help it, couldn't resist it, and the wrongness of it didn't seem to matter. It hadn't even crossed her mind.

By the time she slipped beneath the covers she was in turmoil. In a few minutes she heard him come upstairs. Presently he came out of the bathroom and she heard his door close. She swallowed. Why was her mouth so dry? Was it the champagne? Why did she feel so, so titillated? Golden beads glistened on her breasts in the moonlight. She could feel them on her forehead, she felt flushed. Why was she panting? She closed her eyes and saw his, close and riveting. They drew her into them. She felt like Alice down the rabbit hole. By sheer force of will she blocked out the impression, only to see it replaced by the sight of him lying in bed naked, the sheet angling across his thighs. He was asleep, breathing softly, his chest barely rising. He was beautiful.

She felt her cheeks: too warm. She threw aside the covers and sat on the edge of the bed. At this rate she'd never get to sleep. Go downstairs, brew a pot of tea, sit until she got control, until her thoughts stabilized. This had been a memorable night and now she must forget it; all the looks, the smiles, the touching, the stirring in her heart.

She stood in the doorway. His door, opposite and up the

hall, was no more than six feet away. Walk past it. When she got downstairs, she wouldn't feel this tugging temptation. She pictured electricity crackling unchecked at the end of a parted wire in a storm.

Light showed under his door. Wait until he turns off the lamp. How long would that be? Still flushed, her heart drumming, she took a deep breath and started down the hall. She was across from his door and moved toward it raising both hands, setting them against it and reprising the image of him lying in bed, the sheet across his thighs. She swallowed, closed her eyes and shook her head. This was no good, she had no control.

She didn't realize she was actually leaning against the door until it opened. She fell into his arms. They were kissing, their bodies close. She tingled. In the next moment they were sitting on the bed still clinging. She couldn't let go. With her fingers she framed his face, sliding her hands slowly downward. The tips of her fingers drew in the warmth of his throat, his chest and hard, unyielding stomach that she had felt through his jacket, pressed against his back on the Harley.

A light rain started. Drops struck the outside sill sending up tiny fountains; drops laced the darkened panes. She held him protectingly now, as a mother holds her child in the company of strangers. Her upper body tightened with the wanting to possess him. She lowered her head, pressing her cheek against his chest. How warm he was, how vibrant with life. His heart beat at her cheek as he stroked her hair. She tilted her head back and gazed into his incomparable eyes, seeing sadness. Reluctance? Did this trouble him? Did he feel himself slipping away as she did, and helpless to prevent it?

With hands as soft as velvet he held her face and kissed her, a kiss that went on and on, smoldering, infusing her with fire, a kiss that touched her soul.

She wanted him! It would be wicked, contemptible, and the guilt that followed would rush in like floodwaters to engulf them. Howard would walk in, see their faces, their consciences flaying them, he'd know . . .

She had to stop it. Now! Push him away, get out of there, stay away from him, not touch him, never feel him again, escape before it was too late! He was kissing her cheeks, her throat, her neck up to her ear, pushing through the wall of her resistance, crumbling it.

She struggled with her craving for him, to overcome and subdue it. She tried to drop her arms from around him and rise from the bed but her muscles refused to obey. Like pain suddenly striking, helplessness seized her as he removed her peignoir. It seemed to come to life under its own power. He let it fall and pool on the floor then laid his palms lightly against her breasts, the tips of his index fingers bringing her nipples to erection. Lying back he flung off the covers and eased her down onto him. Her mind reeled, she felt drugged, her muscles refusing to respond to her flagging will, paralyzed, each breath more an effort than the one preceding it. She lay on his chest, their nipples touching, and his eyes took her prisoner.

A thought shot through the craving, causing her to wince. He saw, his expression questioning. He raised her clear of him. She shook her head, dismissing his curiosity, but the thought persisted.

How had they fallen into this quicksand?

No. How had they avoided it this long?

She'd known they were heading for disaster the morning of the water fight. It had started out as horseplay and ended seriously, despite all the laughter. It was a warning she'd ignored.

There were earlier warnings. The day they had lunch after

the incident at the dry-cleaner's, he had picked up the check, she insisted on paying, grabbed his hand and felt an odd tingling sensation. They had looked into each other's eyes. Only a moment, just long enough to silently sound the alarm.

He eased her off him. They lay facing each other. The rain drummed softly, the darkness pushed against the window, blocking the eyes of the world. He kissed her ardently and moved downward, bringing his mouth to her breasts. His tongue began caressing one then the other: licking, stroking, slipping moistly over her flesh. She moaned and trembled as his tongue explored her, bringing a glowing sensation to the surface wherever he touched. He moved effortlessly, finding hollows, crevices, erogenous oases, arousing her.

Her body responded. She sighed long and softly, until she felt wetness. Embarrassment set her tingling. She sensed that he knew, but he didn't move down between her thighs. Instead, he prolonged his assault against her upper body, before slowly, almost casually moving his tongue downward. She moaned, closing her eyes, swinging her head from side to side.

He was above her and lowering. They made love. He was amazing, his desire unsatiable, his energy inexhaustible. In the midst of it she spoke for the first time since entering the room.

"We . . . waited . . . too . . . long . . ."

He gave off a musky scent that intoxicated her, making her wild for him. She suppressed an urge to growl and claw at his flesh, as the room around her blurred and tipped and slowly revolved. She fleetingly thought of the merry-go-round, his hand gripping the upright pole, the strength of his fingers, the latent power. His hand holding the check that day in the restaurant, framing her face minutes before and now holding her tightly against him. The fire ignited, it burned hotter, hotter. It would blaze.

Reined, unrushed, wholly in control, he was a tender lover, giving and sharing. He did not speak, their conversation was tactile, each understanding the other so clearly it was as if they had been lovers for years. They loved and loved, the drumming of the downpour accompanying them and the night stretched into eternity. Hours flew by on wings of incomparable pleasure. In time the rain let up and finally stopped. She could hear it dripping from the eaves, each droplet like the ticking of a clock tracking their ecstasy. Dawn slated the sky. She saw and ignored it, as she did everything in sight; she was too full of him, fixed and focused on him.

He let go of her and sat up turning, setting his feet on the floor. For the first time she got a glimpse of his entire back, the map of his torture. Too late he realized that she could see it and turned back sharply, putting on his robe. When he stood, the backs of his legs showed more abuse.

"What are you getting up for?" she asked.

"It's almost eleven."

She laughed. "Where did the time go?"

She held out her arms beckoning him to her with a rapid motion of her fingers. He bent and kissed her, his musky odor assailing her nostrils.

"I have to go . . ."

"You don't, skip the class."

"I can't, I have a written exam. Besides, aren't you getting up? Aren't you hungry?"

"Famished. For you . . ."

He got back in bed. She held him, glorying in him, and thought about last night. It had been accidental, she'd fallen into his arms. Their willpower deserting them had swept them away. There was no resistance, hesitation. They had gotten too close, dangerously close, submitting without a fight. Love was said to be a game people play; not so, *it was a game that played people.* There was no excuse, they knew what was happening. Love wasn't an alien influence they were ignorant of, it hadn't caught them by surprise.

What neither understood was passion, its power and how weak, how ineffectual people were when threatened by it.

How easily they fell prey to it.

Chapter Twelve

David left the house at 11:45 for an exam on the Old Testament, straight from the arms of his father's wife to the gospels. Cheryl speculated on what must be running through his mind on his way to Columbus. Was he confronting the enormity of their sin? Was he castigating himself? Would he come home wallowing in remorse, his guilt burden heavier than ever?

Curiously, she herself felt only sad about it. For Howard. No regrets, nor remorse. Because it was inevitable? Nothing either of them could have done would have stopped or even slowed the juggernaut. She was deluding herself into thinking she could maintain control. All her efforts had been halfhearted. She didn't want to avoid it, it was that simple. Deep in her heart she had expected this would happen and when it did, when the flower burst into bloom, it would be glorious. It was.

It was almost one o'clock, she was vacuuming the living room. From the moment he left, when she stood at the window watching him roar up the street, her thoughts had been in a maelstrom. No regrets but a lot of anxiety over what was to happen. It was done, they couldn't erase it, couldn't pretend it hadn't happened. Now began the phase she dreaded. He must, too. Adjusting to living with the consequences.

She couldn't close her eyes to the realities. By any yardstick what they'd done was wicked. She'd committed adultery. Where was the guilt? Why wasn't her conscience indicting her? Would it all come, the shame, the self-reproach, the next time she looked into Howard's eyes?

At the moment she felt no shame, she felt awakened; liberated, reborn, the same feeling she'd gotten after riding the

Barbara Riefe

Harley the first time. She remembered denying it when David chided her for living in a shell, challenging her to break out of it. She'd never thought of herself as cloistered but all that had happened since proved that he was right. Was last night the ultimate breakout or willful self-indulgence?

What did the definition matter at this point? What did it matter that her conscience was charitably sparing her? She'd been unfaithful, broken her marriage vow. She remembered how angry she'd been when she thought David had cheated on Angela. She had wanted to physically attack him, she was so enraged.

What irony. He hadn't cheated, then or now. He and Angela were as good as divorced. She wasn't. She remembered what David had said that morning, their conversation while he was getting dressed.

"This had to happen. Everything fell into place to cause it. Some power, some benign and sympathetic god of frustrated lovers ordained it."

"Please, nobody's to blame but us."

"That's not altogether true. Think of what's happened: I come home with Angela, she leaves, Pop is on his rope, the company pulling him in and out of our lives, we're left together at the mercy of temptation. We fight it . . ."

"Did we? I didn't. I saw the blinking red lights and ran through every one."

"Just the same, we didn't exactly jump into bed the minute he was out the door. Besides, whether we fought it or we didn't is irrelevant, it wouldn't have done any good. Forces beyond our control . . ."

"Don't be flippant. I just disagree. I don't buy some god 'ordaining' it."

"Ah, then you believe you control your own destiny."

"I . . ."

132

"*How is that possible? What are any of us but puppets, marionettes? I can't see my strings, I can't feel any but they're there, and somebody else is pulling them.*"

"*Your convenient god. You're saying we're not to blame for our actions. That's much too easy. We're in trouble, David.*"

"*Are we? Will somebody cut out an A and sew it on your forehead? Am I to be pilloried for adultery? People fall in love. It happens. We crashed like two redwoods. Look at me, my darling, look at my lips. I . . . love . . . you. As, God bless her, I never loved Angie. Never loved anybody. You consume me. Our first kiss and the earth dropped from under me. Now my only support is this voluminous, comfortable pink cloud. And up here, closer to the sun the sky is the blue of your eyes.*"

"*Common garden variety blue.*"

"*Beautiful blue. As blue as Ceylonese sapphires, as the waters of the Bashi Channel where it runs into the Pacific. Blame your eyes for all this, they trapped me. I never had a chance. I love you, I've no control, no desire for any. You don't either, is that a crime?*

"*When I was twelve and buying that hideous cat clock for my mother and running around in short pants, and you were sixteen ogling boys and slow dancing to* Love Look Away *and* A Certain Smile, *neither of us knew the other existed. But somebody picked us out of the crowd, manipulated our strings, sent Angie to somebody more her style in a place more to her liking, and left us here, together. According to plan, except . . .*"

" '*Except*'?"

"*Pop. In the way . . .*"

"*Don't put it like that! Don't you dare! You make him sound like an intruder. I love him!*"

"*You love me.*"

"*Him, too.*"

"*Two men at the same time?*"

133

"In different ways, yes."

"I suppose it's possible, if your heart insists." He checked his watch. *"I should go. I'll be back about four."*

She leaned over to vacuum under the piano. The music box lay on the top where she'd left it the night before. She turned off the vac and wound the music box. The *Prelude* played. When the final note struck she closed the lid slowly and kissed it. She resumed vacuuming. She loved his gift and blamed it for everything: it, the evening, the roses. All axes falling, shattering her good intentions.

She was humming "La Adieu" while vacuuming the sofa and didn't hear the Harley coast into the driveway. He burst in, whipping the cord from the wall plug.

"I was in my exam. I said to myself what am I doing here? I broke my record getting home."

"Oh, David . . ."

He kissed her, picked her up and started up the stairs, holding the kiss even while whirling her around on the landing. Moments later, they were naked on top of the covers, kissing, kissing.

The shadows lengthened into late afternoon, the blood-red sun sinking, draping laterally the house across the street. Since coming downstairs her thoughts had been out of control. They sat in the living room having tea, it was too quiet for too long.

"Say it . . ." he murmured.

She avoided his eyes. "We can't go on."

"Yes, we can."

"We can't, we have to end it."

"There's only one way. I leave."

"No!" She nearly upset her cup and saucer in her lap.

"You can't. Don't say it, don't even think it. Promise me."

"Cheryl . . ."

"Promise me!"

"All right, all right."

They sipped in unison. The ormolu clock and the grandfather clock ticked in unison. David studied the rug, his expression morose. It had to be difficult for him, too. All his rationalizing, all his efforts to ease the weight of responsibility, weren't helping either of them. He sat with his eyes downcast, unaware of her staring. It was embarrassing, she couldn't get enough of him. It was like being stricken with an illness that took over body and mind, a malady that consumed your willpower as well as your strength, over which you had no control. Terminal love.

When he sipped his tea the tendon along his jaw drew slightly taut under the flesh. She watched his throat as he swallowed and wanted to slide her fingertips down it. She fixed on his thumb and forefinger holding his cup, crowning the hand that had held her, that excited her so pleasurably every time he touched her. Sunlight sharpened his profile, his head was bowed like Rodin's *Thinker.* She felt an urge to jump up, rush to him, fall on her knees and kiss his hand and neck and throat. He turned to look at her, his expression solemn.

"He comes home tonight."

"Yes."

"I'll pick him up at the airport."

"Yes. This'll be the hard part. I dread it. We'll have to pretend to be relaxed, as if . . ."

"Nothing happened. Only be careful and not overdo it."

"It'll be terribly awkward from now on when he's here, but for you to leave won't solve anything."

"You don't believe that."

"If you leave, I'll die!"

"Cheryl, don't . . ."

"We'll work it out."

"How?"

"There has to be a way. We have to think of him. He can never suspect, David, it would destroy him. He's so proud, such a good husband. He doesn't deserve this . . ."

"*We do?* Cheryl, I love him too, I don't want to hurt him."

It was her fault. She had barged into his room. Looking back, the only real sign he'd given her of his feelings was when he set his hand on her shoulder that day while they were looking at *Luncheon in the Grass*, and that had been nothing more than spontaneous friendly affection. True, his glance betrayed how he felt, but she wasn't meant to see that. She was sure he had no idea his eyes gave him away. She set her cup and saucer down on the piano.

"What do you want for dinner?"

"Three guesses."

"Don't."

"I don't care about dinner, anything'll do. What time is his plane due in?"

"Five fifty-five. You still have half an hour before you need to leave."

He looked appealingly at her. "No! That's all we need. He gets in early, takes a taxi home to surprise me . . . Oh God, David, what . . . are . . . we . . . to . . . do?"

"We can start by keeping our heads."

He came to her and set his hand against her cheek. She held it, kissed it. They kissed.

"One thing you're wrong about," she murmured. "I agree we can't control our destinies, but we're not puppets, we control our actions. At least we should."

"We should if we can. If you parachute from a plane you try not to land in the cactus, but you might."

"You're amazing, so expert at rationalizing. Just please don't ask me to."

He turned from her, "Traffic's murder this time of day, I'd better get going."

Cheryl was taking a roast leg of lamb out of the oven when she heard the car turn into the driveway. She set the pan on a trivet on the counter, closed her eyes, gritted her teeth and exhaled. She took Howard's martini out of the refrigerator, setting it on the counter. He came in grinning, setting his suitcase down, tossing his attache case in a chair, holding out his arms. She kissed him as David looked on then looked away. She put her heart into the kiss; it was serious and sincere. She liked kissing him, she loved him. He responded almost hungrily, then plopped down in a chair.

"What a trip . . . murder!"

"You need a drink."

David spotted his martini and brought it to him. She didn't like that; he hadn't been home two minutes and already they were ganging up on him with kindness. Only what would be the alternative?

He downed half his drink. "Before we sit down to dinner come on up to the observatory."

"The lamb . . ."

"I'll take care of it," said David.

At the top of the attic stairs she grabbed Howard, turning him around, throwing her arms around him, resting her head on his shoulder.

"I wish to God you'd stay home awhile."

"Me, too. What are you going to do?"

"I'm beginning to hate it."

"I know, I know. Any wife would. Any wife as devoted as you are."

She led the way to the telescope. He moved past her and opened the window. It was getting colder, any morning now there would be the first frost. A blast of cold air dried her eyes as he positioned the tube outside.

"We can see Mercury tonight. It's usually hard to see because it can only be observed through a long, turbulent air path. But it's visible now, so says the weather report in the paper."

"The sky's losing its blue."

He peered into the telescope and adjusted it. It took a few seconds to locate the planet and bring it into focus. He talked as he made his adjustments.

"The blue is always variable, even on days when there are no clouds. You probably haven't noticed but the color usually deepens toward the zenith. Most of the time normal blue is diluted with extraneous white light. Fascinating, isn't it? When the sun's directly overhead . . ."

"Howard, you didn't ask me up here to talk about the sun or Mercury."

He had been peering through the lens. He straightened looking suddenly sobered. "You read me like a book. Brace yourself, coming home just now Dave told me everything."

She swallowed lightly, trying, failing to hide it. "What . . . ?"

"He didn't pull any punches, Cheryl. He told me straight out his mind's made up. He's had it with OSU."

"My God, I mean . . . he's not dropping out?"

"He is. It's definite." His eyes ignited. "Don't you get it, he's giving me a second chance! Before he enrolls somewhere else I'll have another crack at it. Oh, when he told me I didn't mention the job, the company, nothing. But talk about heaven-sent opportunities . . ."

"Dropping out."

"Now won't be like when we kicked it around the first time. I made a mess of that. I was overeager. Now he's been home awhile, we've developed a relationship. Since Angela left we've become friends. Oh, not like you two, but he opens up to me now where before he didn't at all."

She peered through the telescope to keep from showing her distress. Mercury was a yellow thumbprint on the lens. Her heart beat faster, her breath came in gasps, she couldn't control. He'd changed his mind! He was leaving after all, his promise be damned! Without a word to her he'd arbitrarily decided this was the best course, his escape hatch. How dare he!

"Let's go back down," she murmured.

"First get a good look at Mercury, it's not the easiest planet to . . ."

"The hell with Mercury!"

"What's the matter?"

"Nothing, I'm sorry. I did see it, it's got a yellowish tinge. Howard, let's please go back down. If the lamb overcooks it'll be dry and stringy."

David had put the lamb back in the oven and turned down the heat. It was moist and delicious. The evening was awkward and electric. She could see that David's conscience was stretching him on the rack. Was it belated misgivings or changing his mind about leaving and not telling her? Howard did his best but finally gave up trying to keep the conversation enjoyable, retreating into recounting his trip. Cheryl and he went upstairs early. The lamp wasn't out thirty seconds when he rolled over, easing his arm across her.

"Missed you."

"I missed *you*. Like I said, I'm getting to hate it."

"Me, too."

"I hope you're home for awhile."

"I do, too. These days there's so many balloons in the air, I don't know where I'll be one week to the next. It used to be I could schedule almost the whole month. No more."

He kissed her and began foreplay. She did her best, trying to concentrate and respond. It was impossible. The problem was simple and glaringly obvious: she didn't want *him* making love to her. She slipped into pretending he was David holding her, but quickly gave up on that. It was useless, they were nothing like each other. Howard tried but too hard; it showed, he was tense, too calculated, too predictable. No spontaneity, no surprises, and David had done things that in Howard's wildest imagination he would never have attempted.

David finished *The Song of Solomon* and closed his Bible. He put out the light and lay back. It wasn't Solomon or the song of songs he thought about, it was Solomon's mother and David's adultery with her. David stood on his roof looking down on Bathsheba washing herself and was struck by her beauty. He asked about her. Eventually he arranged for her to be brought to him and lay with her. She conceived. David was informed. Her husband, Uriah the Hittite, one of David's captains, became an obstacle. David sent a letter to Uriah, ordering him to the forefront of the "hottest" battle in the war against the Ammonites. Uriah was killed; Bathsheba mourned her husband, and when the mourning passed, David took her as his wife. She bore a son, Solomon.

"And the Lord was displeased . . ."

Chapter Thirteen

Howard had to stop off at the doctor's for a blood pressure check before going to work. He left the house half an hour early. Minutes after he drove away, Cheryl went up to David's room. She stood at the door reining in her anger, then knocked.

"Come in."

He shifted to one side of the bed, lifting the covers and patting beside him.

"Never mind, you and I have to talk. You lied, you gave me your word you wouldn't leave."

"What did he tell you?"

"What did you tell him?"

"Let's backtrack. If you remember, Cheryl, you said we could work this out, that there has to be a solution. Well I've wrung my feeble brain till its limp and the only solution I can see is the obvious one: I leave. Last night, while I was waiting for Pop's plane at the airport, I called one of my professors, Dr. Steele. He had told me about a school in New Mexico."

"New Mexico? Good God!"

"Let me go on. It's near a place called Arroyo, north of Taos. It's not a seminary but religion is all they teach . . ."

"I don't want to hear this." She started for the door.

"At least let me explain why I didn't tell you . . ."

She turned, clapping her hands over her ears. "No! I don't care!"

"I'm sorry."

"You're 'sorry,' that helps."

"Come here, sit beside me."

"No, damnit. Damn you!"

She slammed the door behind her and went down to the

living room, resentful and angry. How could he do this? Tear her heart out! Talk about it so dispassionately, without any sense at all of the pain he was inflicting?

Did he have classes that day or had he already dropped out of school? What did it matter, it was over, he was out the door. She looked over at the roses on the end table. One had dropped a petal. They looked lifeless, they were dying. Too soon.

He hung around all morning. They tried to avoid each other. It got to be farcical—when one walked into a room, the other walked out. When he went out without telling her where or when he'd be back, her anger deserted her. She sat down and cried. She'd held it in all morning. She caught herself when the phone rang.

"Cheryl?" It was Howard. "Good news. My blood pressure's flirting with normal. Mills is so pleased, he's taking me off the pills."

"Great! Only why didn't you call me before you left his office?"

"In too big a rush. Things have been popping around here ever since I walked in. Dear . . ."

"What?"

"I'm afraid I have to run down to Memphis."

"Wonderful!"

"I'm sorry. The thing is I'll have to leave from here, company limo. I don't want you to be without a car for three days."

"Three . . ."

"I'm sorry. Anyway, Dave could pick up the car, pile his motorcycle in the trunk and drive home. He won't mind."

"How did all this Memphis business happen so suddenly?"

"It's a little complicated over the phone but it's a big deal, huge. The thing is I'll be needing my suitcase. Can you or Dave bring it to the airport? My flight is . . . hold on . . . , three forty-two. It's already after one, which makes it a little tight."

"Howard, how am I supposed to get to the airport? By taxi? There are only two in town and you can never reach either when you really need one."

"You're right. Damn . . ." There was a pause. "Tell you what, I'm stuck here in meetings till the limo picks me up, but I'll have Myra get one of the kids from the mailroom to drive our car home. He can catch a bus back. How's that?"

"Whatever . . ."

"You're upset. I'm really, really sorry."

"It's not your fault."

"I'll get right on the car, he should be there in no time. It'll give you time to pack my bag. Boy, am I lucky this isn't one of your library days."

"You'll have your suitcase, don't worry about it."

"Thanks, dear, you're terrific. Is Dave around?"

"He went out. Who knows when he'll be back."

"Has he said anything about dropping out of school?"

"He . . . let's not get into that now, okay? Just get the car back here so I can get to the airport in time for your flight."

"I will, I will."

"Good."

Howard was waiting for her by the window that over-looked the short-term parking lot. They exchanged waves when she got out of the car.

He welcomed her, his arms wide. "That's my girl." His grin sagged. "You're still upset, aren't you? I don't blame you."

"I'm not upset. Just, I don't know, tired. Rough day. I'm going home and lounge in the tub."

"If it's any consolation, I hate doing things this way. I like everything scheduled down to the minute."

"I know, Howard."

He checked his watch against the overhead clock. "Look at that, it's still off. Three minutes. You'd think somebody would have the pride and the professionalism to ride herd on the time of day around this dump!"

She agreed. She saw him off and drove home. David was back. When she walked in he was sitting on the living room floor using the coffee table as a desk. On it was a stamped manila envelope and papers neatly laid out. He was signing them.

"From Angie's lawyer. She gets her divorce, I get free postage." He folded the papers mock-ceremoniously and placed them in the envelope. "So now I'm a free man."

"Congratulations."

"You're still sore. Can we talk about it?"

"Why bother? We'll only end up at each other's throats. Do what you want, go to New Mexico, go to the South Pole, for all I care."

"I've been accepted but I haven't called the school yet. If it means anything, that's the reason I held off telling you."

"So call, what are you waiting for?"

"What do you think?"

He rose to his feet. They stood staring at each other. She ran to his arms.

"I hate this, David. . . ."

He held her from him, searching her eyes. "Listen to me, you were right after all, there is a solution. It's the only way. I leave, you come with me."

She turned away, her mind whirling. She turned back.

"You know I can't. It's not possible. You're not serious."

"I'm dead serious. Look at me, we have two choices. We

can do it your way: I stay and this hell on earth goes on and on until one of us stumbles with Pop. Or we leave." She started to speak. He set a finger against her lips. "No, don't say a word, not yet. Sleep on it. It's the solution, Cheryl, but you'll have to decide. I can't twist your arm. I can't in conscience even sell you. But I have faith in you, faith in the strength of our love. You'll come with me. I know you will."

Chapter Fourteen

Even during lovemaking that night, Cheryl felt torn and tormented. David said nothing further about their leaving together, he didn't talk about Howard. He'd said nothing against him, but he wouldn't. It wouldn't have persuaded her to desert him. How could she? What an almighty mess!

David went off to classes, his final day at OSU. He made arrangements to forward his grades and saw to all the other details needed to effect his transfer. When he came home late that afternoon, it was to an empty house. Cheryl worked until six. He prepared dinner. They went to bed early.

He woke her with a kiss the next morning. She extricated herself from his arm and sat up.

"You're leaving today . . ."

She could see "we" forming on his lips but he didn't articulate it.

"Tomorrow, I still have a few loose ends." She looked away feeling wretched. "I'll be tied up most of the morning. I have to take the Harley in to the dealer for a tune-up. It's around fourteen hundred miles to Arroyo. So . . ." He took her in his arms searching her eyes. "Have you decided?"

"I can't do it, I can't leave with you."

"You want to."

"I can't."

"But you're still mulling it over?"

"I . . . I'm not."

"Remember the day we went to the park, the day the little boy spilled his ice cream? You tried for the brass ring and missed." He held her, gazing into her eyes. "It's coming around again. Don't miss it this time. It's not a free ride,

146

Cheryl, it's your life, the next sixty years. I love you, I want to be with you forever."

"Please. Don't you think I haven't thought about the future? About everything? Over and over? Get up, get dressed, take the Harley in. I . . . need more time to think."

He brightened. "You *are* thinking, that's good, that's very good. It's all I ask."

She got up. "I have to take a shower. Breakfast'll be ready in half an hour."

She found it impossible to get to sleep that night. His deadline was a phantom haunting her. He would leave and they'd never see each other again. These golden hours together, their brief happiness was a brief candle. Lit, it burned steadily, bringing light and comfort, warmth to her heart; only to melt, gutter and die in a wisp of smoke tomorrow. She looked over at him still asleep. His breath came effortlessly, the covers rising and falling. He was beautiful, she wanted to hold his face, stare and stare, drink in his dark handsome beauty like nectar. He had Howard's dark hair and gray eyes but the design was sleeker, more compact and muscular. Over and above love he gave her life. She fed off him, off his spirit, his confidence and boldness facing the future.

What would her life be after he dropped out of it? Would it revert to what it had been? She couldn't believe that, not the way she'd changed. What about Howard? Dear, dependable, lovable Howard, anchor and rock? Willing to do anything to make her happy, except to give her up. To his own flesh and blood? Worse than heartless, that would be sadistic. He'd already lost Lydia, now for her to walk out on him, with his son . . . Unthinkable!

It was nearing one in the afternoon. The Harley stood in

the driveway, the saddlebags packed, the tank full. They stood in the foyer. David was ready to leave.

"You're coming, my darling. I can wait, there's time, we're not bound by the clock. You're coming, you know you are."

"Don't . . ."

"What, tempt you? I wish I could give you my eyes for just ten seconds so you could see yourself: your eyes, your jaw line, how taut it is, your body, how you're standing. You've decided. Your heart has, it just hasn't told your brain yet. I can wait."

"I can't do it to him."

"You can only have one of us, Cheryl. You know you want to come. You're not tempted to, it's past that, you have to. Only your sense of loyalty is holding you back."

"Not true. I love him, David."

"You love me so that's a wash. If you made two lists, a lot evens out between us. What it all boils down to is the rest of your life. Holland Springs, the library, Mavis Delaney, dropping him off and picking him up at the airport, a routine as predictable as the sunrise. Or what we can have, what we can make of our life together."

She turned from him. Howard was love. He gave so much so freely it opened her heart to pour out all that she felt for him, all that he aroused. When he held her before they made love, before they kissed, and she looked at him, in his expression she could see his devotion, the earnestness in his eyes. It went deeper than devotion, in his desire to please he subjugated himself to her. I'm here to serve you, to make you happy. Dismiss your worries, your fears and doubts. Here in the fortress of my arms you're safe. As I am in yours. You fulfill me. Howard, Howard . . .

And David. His table offered the same, only added excitement. Their forays into passion and the booty, the afterglow of gratification. How they consumed her! Howard was cozy slippers on a winter night. Howard was a sturdy house against wind and storm. David was the fire in the grate that set her blazing with him. He was adventure, he was challenge. Even the uncertainty of what lay ahead appealed to her, beginning with not even knowing where they'd stop that night.

If she went with him. If she did they'd be striking out into the unknown, in a less than stalwart ship in unpredictable weather, sailing too near the wind. No assurances, no guarantees, life would overwhelm them at times . . .

She still avoided his eyes. He was wrong, it wasn't "past temptation." He was a rope around her waist pulling her toward him. Away from Howard.

"I want to come," she whispered.

"You have to. Because you love me."

"Fiercely. It scares me. I see us inside each other on a bearskin in front of a roaring fire. Outside, a blizzard is howling, the sun is a cold cinder, the whole world is arctic. Inside, you're the fire, crackling, blazing."

"You can't leave it."

"Only to leave him would be heartless. Humiliating for him. And so selfish . . ."

"Cheryl, this is not about him or me, it's all you. There's no question it takes guts. It took guts for you to get on the Harley the first time, to kiss me . . ."

"Please."

Both clocks struck one. He glanced at his watch.

"Pack your bags."

She stood at the door looking past him at the horizon joining two houses across the street. A solitary maple stood midway between them, blocking the way. She pictured the tree being cut down, the obstacle removed. She turned back to him.

"How do we carry my two suitcases?"

"I'll phone the express agency. We can leave them outside the door to be picked up. They'll probably get to New Mexico before we do." He held her, kissed her. "Go on up."

She nodded.

He set both suitcases outside.

"The express agency says they'll pick them up, no problem. The truck's making the rounds. They'll pick up here sometime later this afternoon. Are you ready?"

"I have to leave a note."

"Of course."

He waited while she sat at the kitchen table and composed a note. She wrote six, crumpling them all. Two more failed attempts followed. David came in.

"Problems?"

"I don't know how to say it, it's so shocking, so cold."

"Cheryl . . ."

"What?"

"I honestly don't think it'll be a shock to him."

"You think he knows? God! I can't believe that. He would have said . . ."

"That's true, but neither of us'll win an Oscar for acting. It is possible that by now he's beginning to sense it. Maybe you're trying too hard to sugarcoat the note. Tell him the truth and tell him you'll phone him."

"That's another thing, when neither of us shows up at the airport tomorrow and he calls and nobody answers he'll have to take a taxi. Of course he's done that before."

"A short note, two sentences. I know it's not easy, but you pull a sliver out, you don't ease it."

"Yes."

She wrote the note, folded it and set a magnet against

it on the refrigerator door.

"All set?"

She went into the living room and looked around. He came to her, squeezing her hand encouragingly.

"I guess . . ."

He stood aside. She started for the door. The phone rang. They reacted, exchanging glances. She went into the kitchen to pick it up, he followed.

"Cheryl? Success, success! We knocked 'em for a loop! Signed, sealed and delivered a day ahead of schedule, how about that? I used up all my luck on this one! I'm heading home. I'll be in at . . . wait, wait . . . four-twenty, flight two-oh-six. Tonight, my love, we celebrate. Big time! The three of us. Dinner, a night on the town. Four twenty . . ."

"Howard . . ."

"I gotta get off. Bye."

"Howard . . ." She turned to David. "He hung up."

She kept her hand against the phone back in its cradle. She looked around wistfully at the familiar, her kitchen, her home.

"He'll be all right, he'll be fine." David nodded to strengthen the assurance.

"I don't think so."

"Are you ready?"

She hesitated, finding her lower lip with her teeth, scraping it lightly. One last look around.

"Mmmm . . ."

Chapter Fifteen

The mostly commercial traffic was relatively light early in the afternoon. They skirted Columbus to the north heading westnorthwest, getting onto Route 270 and taking a left at New Rome onto Route 40. By this time, Cheryl was feeling at peace with herself. It was her fourth time on the Harley. It charged her as usual but the curtain drawn between them before had been torn away by their intimacy. Now the closeness brought lurid thoughts of his body and hers joined, inseparable. The speed, the wind, the freedom sharpened her senses. She felt vibrantly alive.

He had mapped a route that would take them through Indianapolis, Springfield, Kansas City, and eventually down to Wichita and across to the northern boundary of New Mexico.

She clung to him, indulging in him. The landscape flew by, the wind tore at them, they seemed to soar, the roar of raw power between their legs muffling as they rose. He was a free spirit making her as free as he was. No spirits were freer than they. The thirties dulled the fine edge, the forties stifled free spirits, the liberty of action, the latitude, were lost. Or thrown away. Only the young were truly free.

They were free. She wanted to shout for joy!

Until her conscience shouted first.

David accelerated, roaring past a semi, getting back into line behind a shimmying RV. Cars flew by in the opposite direction heading for Columbus, for the suburbs, Holland Springs. She leaned to one side.

"Pawling coming up," he shouted over his shoulder.

"Pull over . . ."

"Something wrong?"

"Pull over. Stop."

The Harley ground gravel as he slowed along the apron.
The semi they had passed and the cars following it tore by as
he stopped. She let go of him and got off. He kicked down the
stand, his expression grim.

"You can't go on. Can't do this to him, devastate his self-
esteem. Humiliate him, destroy his ego . . ."

"None of the above. You're talking pity, that's not it. It's
love, David. Attachment. He and I are connected. I feel the
band stretching and the further away we get, the tauter it gets.
We could go to the end of the earth and it wouldn't snap. Distance only strengthens it, so I'm finding out."

She paused. Both studied the gravel at their feet. Why go
on explaining? Why drag it out unnecessarily? He toed the
gravel and picked up a stone, throwing it into the grass-lined
ditch paralleling the highway. The rush of air from traffic
rocked them where they stood. He looked away then back at
her, smiling gamely. Cars and trucks continued to scream by,
the end of the world was only moments away, and there she
stood on an unfamiliar highway crushing the loveliest rose
she had ever held.

"I'll take you back," he finally said.

"You don't have to. We'll go on to Pawling, I'll catch a bus
back to Columbus and a taxi home. David . . ."

"Yes?"

"For what it's worth, I'm dying to come with you."

"Cheryl . . ."

"Please. I'll die tonight when I wake up and you're not
there and I know that you'll never be again. But if I go, by
sundown I'll be miserable. I won't be fit to live with. You'd
run out of patience with me before we got halfway to New
Mexico. I can't do that to either of us. As I say, it's this tie
pulling me back. It's just too strong, too strong."

She had been avoiding his eyes. Now she looked at them

and it felt as if the life that he'd given her, the freedom, was seeping from her pores, leaving her empty. The free spirit dies here. Sight of him dimmed as tears welled in her eyes. "I'll miss you horribly. Everything about you, all that we have. I'll . . ."

She stopped and waved away further words. She got back on the Harley. They roared back onto the highway. Minutes later he pulled into the Pawling bus station. The terminal resembled an oversized barn, only with a corrugated iron roof. It threatened ramshackle. Four elderly men shared a bench outside, chewing, gossiping, taking in the October sun. Two buses had pulled in, passengers were getting off the nearest one. The other sat empty. About three quarters of the vehicles in the parking lot were pickup trucks. David nodded toward a phone booth.

"I'll call the express agency, tell them to cancel the order to pick up the suitcases. You'd better check on buses."

Schedules filled a wooden rack attached to the wall near the station door. She selected one and ran a finger down the list of times. There was a 2:06 bus, four stops to downtown Columbus. She could get a taxi at the terminal. She'd have ample time to get home, change her clothes and get out to the airport. Through the front window she could see the clock over the ticket seller's barred window. The minute hand clicked to two o'clock. David hung up the phone and walked toward her.

"I caught them on their way out. The suitcases'll be there when you get home."

"I can make a two-oh-six."

He offered money. "You'll need this . . ."

"I have enough, thanks. Wait for me. Don't leave, please don't . . ."

Inside, the waiting room looked like pews in a church.

Couples and individuals sat in varying stages of consciousness. A woman leaned against her companion's shoulder snoring. A burly red-haired man in bib overalls fought the cigarette machine for his matches. Two little girls played a shrill game of tag, ignoring their mothers shushing. The ticket seller's crew cut looked like a crowd of golden needles as he lowered his head to fish change out of his drawer.

"Is it usually on time?"

"Nice day like today, 'twill be."

She went back outside. David leaned against the Harley, his arms folded. She walked toward him. He looked destroyed. She was the destroyer. She couldn't have made a worse botch of it, agreeing to come after all that soul-searching and then changing her mind. Up the highway a bus dwarfed cars and pickup trucks. He turned and followed her eyes. When he faced her again, his expression was so sad it tugged at her heart. Now would come the hardest of all, the nettling remorse, even second thoughts, she would surely suffer all the way back to Holland Springs.

"Do you remember the day we talked over the picnic table in the woods? The bird overhead on the branch of that tree?" he murmured.

"The beech tree."

"And earlier, when we didn't speak to each other all morning and I finally left the house. I went out there. I carved a heart in that tree with your initials and mine. You can't see it from the table, it's around the other side where nobody can see it. I figured that whatever happened to us, and things were looking pretty bleak that day, we'd at least have something permanent to show where we'd been, what happened, how we fell in love."

"Oh, David."

He grinned uncomfortably. "We didn't make it but the

heart will. Beeches grow very old."

The bus came. The brakes released pressure, the driver opened the door.

"Can we kiss good-bye?" he asked.

"Of course."

It was not the kiss she'd become accustomed to: no fire, scarcely even warmth. Her fault, she held back and broke it too soon, not wanting to remember it all the way home. Two passengers got off the bus. The loudspeaker above the terminal entrance blared, inviting passengers to board, listing the stops and announcing departure time. David had gotten her overnight bag out of the saddlebag.

"Good-bye, Cheryl, have a good life."

He was crying, she could see. She squeezed his forearm comfortingly and loved him, loved him.

"You, too."

"You and Pop both. You will. He's a good man, a good husband. Tell him . . ." He looked off. "Never mind, who am I to tell him anything?"

"Good-bye."

She wanted to hug him, she resisted doing so. He got on the Harley, turned it over, took off, waving once without looking back and leaving a steadily ascending plume of hazel-colored dust against the blue, blue sky.

It wasn't until Cheryl was turning into the driveway with Howard beside her that she remembered the note left on the refrigerator. Running in earlier to change her clothes and unpack the suitcases, she hadn't even thought of it. She could feel her cheeks pale. Howard was talking, David's leaving had sapped some of his happiness over his success in Memphis.

"I don't know why he couldn't hang around until I got back, to say good-bye," he said for the fourth or fifth time.

"What's a couple hours for a trip that long? Mr. Impulsive, out of OSU and into whatever-it's-called. Worst of it is I never got a chance to even bring up the job, though I guess if he was interested he would have mentioned it. I couldn't talk him into it the first time, what makes me think . . . oh hell, forget it. Let me have one martini, give me time to freshen up and we'll drive into the city and have dinner. It's early, maybe catch a movie first . . ."

"We don't have to eat out. I've got two perfectly good steaks, plenty of vegetables. I can make dinner in an hour. You can help."

"Me, in the kitchen? Are you kidding?"

"You in the kitchen. From now on."

"I can't even boil water."

"It's not complicated. Seriously, why should we be in separate rooms when we can be together enjoying each other's company?"

"What's gotten into you?"

"Well, doesn't it make sense?"

She tensed as she remembered the note. She gently pushed ahead of him as they went in the side door.

"Mix your martini, put on some music."

"Look at your roses, Cheryl, they're all dead." They had dropped nearly half their petals since the last time she looked. "Want me to throw them out?"

"I will. First I'll get dinner started."

"I'm helping."

"When I call you. Sit and relax."

She made a beeline for the kitchen, snatching the envelope in stride, crumpling it and tossing it in the trash basket under the sink just as Howard entered.

"I said I'd call you . . ."

Her hand was shaking. She shoved it behind her back.

"Okay, okay, I just need ice for the shaker."

They enjoyed a long, leisurely dinner. He told her all about Memphis, practically from touch-down to take-off. He was very proud without bragging. After dinner they watched television. She sat watching and not watching, feeling she needed a bath. Scrub and scrub and scrub away the day. Only it would be a long time before it rubbed off, if ever. It was after ten-thirty when he started up the stairs.

"Coming . . . ?"

"In a bit, I need a cup of tea."

"Are you all right?"

"Of course, why wouldn't I be?"

"I don't know, you seem a little . . . down. Is it Dave's leaving?"

"I'll miss him."

"You got to be close. Good friends."

"Good friends."

"I'll miss him, too. I'll have to find another golf partner. Cheer up, maybe this time he'll keep in touch. He might even come back to visit, you think?"

"Maybe."

"You don't think."

"We'll see, won't we? Wait . . ." She walked up to him, put his arms around her and kissed him. He reacted pleased. "Don't you dare fall asleep on me."

"Oh, that sounds promising . . ."

He went up. While the water heated for tea, she brought the roses out to the kitchen to dispose of them, one by one, down to the last fallen petal. They hadn't lasted long, not even a week.

She had almost finished her second cup of tea when she got up from the table, went to the cabinet in the living room and got out the music box. It was already wound. She sat in the kitchen, opened the top and listened to the pretty strains of the "Prelude in D flat."

She sipped and listened and set her cup down. The second time through the melody, the spring winding down, a tear rolled down her cheek and dropped softly into her tea.

Epilogue

Cheryl's fingers danced lightly and flawlessly through "The Minute Waltz." It was early on a sultry Saturday afternoon. She was tempted to put on the air conditioner but four days into summer seemed far too early to capitulate to the heat. Howard in his work clothes came in from the back porch sweating, going straight to the clock to adjust it to his watch. She smiled as she looked at the photograph of the two of them on the mantle to the right of his back. Married thirty-one years, retired and still worshipping at the altar of punctuality.

"How's the back door coming?"

"Just getting started. I'll need a new blade for the plane. I need wood screws, too. Hanscom's Hardware has a sale in today's paper, a set of socket wrenches for thirty percent off."

"Do you need socket wrenches?"

"Mine are shot. I'm missing two. It's a helluva sale, I hate to pass it up. Aren't you hot in here? I should turn on the air conditioner."

"It's not that bad. We'd have to close all the windows and you're in and out. Let's hold off a week or so. You should phone Hanscom's, make sure they have the socket wrenches in stock."

"Why would they advertise them if they don't have any?"

"Well change those pants before you leave the house."

"Hey, they're used to seeing me down there like this. Do you need anything in town?"

"There's dry cleaning but I can pick it up Monday."

"I can pick it up . . ."

"No, I've a bone to pick with the manager. Your dress

shirts came back with the sleeves wrinkled."

"I'll give him hell."

"*I'll* talk to him. You just pay attention to driving."

"You always say that, I always do."

She laughed. "Because I always say that. And don't be too late getting back. We're due at the Macombers at seven-thirty and we have to stop by and pick up the Carters."

"Another party?"

"We're going to have to give one of our own."

"We just had one," he said.

"That was a different crowd."

She could hear him backing out of the driveway as she resumed playing. She swept through "The Minute Waltz" a third time then segued into "L'Adieu." She paused part way through it. Through the window she saw an Army surplus jeep, a relic that looked as if it had never been washed, pull up in front of the house. The tires looked recapped with mud, the canvas top was down. The driver got out. He stood surveying the house. She went to the door and watched him come up the walk. He was tall, broad-shouldered, in his fifties; his shoulder-length hair was gray, his full beard the same color only speckled white. It wasn't until he was about six paces from her and turned from inspecting the lawn to look straight at her, their eyes meeting for the first time, that she recognized him. She gasped and pushed open the screen door.

"David!"

"Cheryl . . ."

He squeezed her hands. A tingling ran up her arms. She held the door open for him. In the foyer they stood a foot apart staring at each other. Her heart pounded. Nearly thirty years! She smoothed her skirt self-consciously and raised a hand to her cheek. They continued to stare as he attempted a smile. It flicked a switch, pulling up the past, jumbled and blurred scenes flying by: getting on the Harley, turning to look back at the suitcases on the stoop, the house, the road beckoning invitingly, promising a whole new life, exciting, colorful. He spoke, erasing the images, blanking the screen.

"You . . . look the same."

"Not counting the glasses, the touch-up on my hair, the wrinkles and lines, the years . . ."

"So many."

"Twenty-nine. And not a word from you. Not a phone call, a card. Why only twenty-nine, why not forty or fifty? I should be mad as hell!"

"I know. You've every right to be. You can't imagine how many times I picked up the phone and put it down again. Started to write a card and stopped."

"The least you could have done was let us know you were alive."

"I . . . wanted to, but . . ."

"What?"

"I worried that I might have left behind a problem. I had no way of knowing what he knew. It was like moving from one campsite to the next, you just let the old fire die."

"He didn't know a thing. I never told him. I didn't . . . have the guts."

"You didn't have the heart."

"Half and half, I guess."

"Only as I say, I had no way to know that. Besides, if you think about it, wasn't a clean break better? Like when Angie left? She just dropped out of our lives."

"She was different. That was different. I should still be furious with you!"

"Only you're not."

Talking, explaining seemed to relax him. Onto his face

came his old smile: full, glorious, stirring her heart as it had back then, half a lifetime ago. Her annoyance passed.

"Aren't you going to ask me in?"

She laughed. "No."

"Are you okay?"

"A little dizzy. Delayed reaction or something. Come in, come in."

He looked about the living room. He seemed a stranger seeing it for the first time. It was understandable.

"Everything's changed," she said.

"Except the piano."

"The whole house is changed. You should see what your father did to the attic. Mount Palomar on Warren Avenue. And two years ago we had a whole new kitchen installed." She sensed she was beginning to rattle. Why did everybody assume babbling concealed nervousness when it was just the opposite? And any second now her hands would begin flying about out of control. "Come and see the kitchen."

On the way he glanced at the Wedgewood vase filled with tulips.

She smiled. "The roses died."

In the kitchen he looked around. "Very nice." He wasn't the least bit interested. "How've you been?"

"Okay, no complaints. You?"

"Great, great . . ."

They were back to staring at each other. Another ten seconds of this and she'd resume babbling about the changes in the house. He seemed just as edgy.

"Is Pop . . . all right?"

"Fine. You just missed him. He went into town to get something at the hardware store."

"Is it still Melville's? Driving through, I didn't notice."

"It's been Hanscom's for fifteen years. Sit." Suddenly, inexplicably, she wanted to set her hand against his upper arm, to assure him he was welcome, that she was pleased and happy to see him. She held back. He might misunderstand. "How about some iced tea? It won't take but a minute. No wait, you want milk."

"Nothing, thanks."

She was glad he declined a drink. It would mean they'd have to sit opposite each other. Back would come memories of dark hours when Howard slept and they sat opening their secret doors to each other and growing irrevocably closer. He leaned against the sink pretending interest in each major appliance in turn. He looked as thin as when he drove up with Angela that first day. Not pasty like then, though, now his cheeks above his beard were ruddy. He nodded at the plain white clock above the sink.

"I see your favorite cat finally ran out of lives. In your whole life have you ever seen a tackier clock?"

"Twelve-year-old taste."

"How do you remember I was twelve?"

"There's little I don't remember." She touched her forehead between her eyes. "It's all bunched together separate and apart from everything else."

"It's the same with me. As soon as I saw the turn-off sign for Holland Springs that day started coming back bit by bit, everything we did from the time we left here."

Silence. They were back to staring. Both looked away at the same time.

"This is quite a surprise," she murmured.

"Don't you mean shock? Are you sorry I came, Cheryl?"

"Of course not."

She pulled out a chair for him and sat down opposite, resolving to take her chances. Hopefully, having brought it up and dropped it, he wouldn't rehash 'that day' in detail. It was painful. He continued to stand gripping the back of the chair, leaning against it.

"I apologize for not calling ahead to warn you, only if Pop answered the phone . . . I know you said he doesn't know a thing, but . . ."

"You couldn't be sure."

"I don't want to hurt either of you."

The clock ticked, she could faintly hear a plane passing over.

"Where have you come from?" she asked. "Where are you heading?"

"Before I get to that can I ask you a loaded question? On the way home from Pawling, any . . . regrets?"

"Yes." It was the answer he wanted, he looked pleased. "You went on to your school . . ."

"Ryerson."

"How did it go?"

"Better than OSU. What I learned justified my transferring. I graduated, took my degree to Berkley and got my master's."

"What became of the Harley?"

"I rode it into the ground and sold it for junk."

No surprise but still disappointing. Every so often she thought about the Harley, how, tempted by his challenge, she'd dared to get on it the first time. How the freedom of the open road it symbolized had helped influence her, and how close she'd come to running to New Mexico into a whole new life.

"You teach . . ."

"Taught. At a small college in Oregon: Wellington. Like the Duke. You've never heard of it, nobody has."

Things had not turned out as he expected.

"I naively thought that at least some of my students would

be interested. I found you have to generate interest, not take it for granted. The best laid plans . . ."

"You quit?"

"I stuck it out for six years. In the meantime I started writing articles for religious publications. I found that I liked writing, especially the research. Eventually, I was able to support myself with my writing. I've been at it eighteen years."

"What sort of articles?"

"Not tracts, no daily prayers or inspirational stuff. Subjects Biblical scholars would be interested in. I just sent in a monograph on Paul's epistle to the Galatians. It deals with how Martin Luther found it useful in developing Lutheranism." He laughed thinly. "I specialize in subjects other religious writers don't bother with; secret of my limited success."

"Where are you going from here?"

"New York. To fly to England, Cambridge. I'm psyched. It's a juicy assignment. I'll be there two years. Clive Holbrook taught at Magdalene College. Remember Clive, the Sty, Woodrow, the escape? *My* escape. Not his. Anyway, at that time his parents were living in Cambridge. He also had two younger sisters. Somebody must still be around I can talk to. The university is remarkable. Isaac Newton taught math there, the library has three million volumes. They may need the Marines to get me out of the stacks after my two years are up."

She set her hands flat on the table pretending to examine her nails. "Are you married?"

No sooner did she say it then she intuitively knew he was not; what wife would let her husband run off by himself for two years? Why even ask? It was presumptuous, only he didn't seem to resent it.

"No, I haven't come close. Not that I haven't met any-body, but all daisies."

" 'Daisies'?"

"Or marigolds. In my garden there was only one rose."

She looked out the windows over the sink. When she looked back at him, she got the impression he regretted having said it. He quickly changed the subject.

"How's Pop's health? Listen to me, I'm fifty-three, what I mean is how is Howard's health?"

"Excellent, for seventy-three. He keeps fit, he still has a thirty-four inch waist. His blood pressure's under control without pills. The company made him CEO in 1985."

"Good for him."

"He deserved it, he devoted his life to Great Lakes Re. He retired five years ago."

"Does he keep busy?"

"Very. I saw to that the year he retired. I bought him a set of home handyman books for his birthday. He fixes *every-thing.*"

"That's funny. When I was here he barely knew one end of a hammer from the other."

"You know him, anything he tackles he's not satisfied until he's expert. He's on his fifth telescope. It's about the most powerful one you can buy."

"Does he still drag you up to the attic to look through it?"

"The observatory. Yes. He can even take pictures with this one. Please don't get him started on it."

"I see you've got a two-car garage now. Two cars. Are you still at the library?"

"No, I gave it up the day after you left. I decided it was contributing to the rut I was in. I got my old bookkeeping job back with Clifton, Adams and Drury."

They heard the front door open and close.

"Damn fools! Who the hell advertises a sale and runs out of the merchandise halfway through the first day? I gave Neil Hanscom a piece of my mind, you bet. Did you see that junk parked in front of the house?"

David went into the living room, she followed. Howard turned from pointing at the jeep. His jaw sagged, his eyes rounded, a grin slowly developed.

"Dave!" He threw his arms around him then held him away. "Will you look at this guy? What's with the Shredded Wheat? It's the old man of the mountain, Cheryl. Hey, this is terrific! What a surprise!"

"You look great, Howard."

"Hey, your old man takes care of himself. Tiptop shape, that's me. Look at him, Cheryl, talk about a sight for sore eyes. Thirty years and not a whisper. How are we supposed to know if you're dead or alive?"

"Sorry, it just seemed better that way."

"I don't follow you there but hey, here you are, safe and sound. How about something cold to drink? Maybe some of that Minnesota fudge cake? Cheryl?"

"Give me a minute."

"Sit!" boomed Howard, plumping down on the sofa. "Not there, here beside me. Let's have a good look. God Almighty, you're a rail, we'll have to stuff you full of steak. Cheryl, call up the folks and cancel tonight. We're not leaving this house. We've got hours and hours of catching up here. Thirty years. Goddamn, half a lifetime. Hey, you *are* staying . . ."

"I'd love to but I can't."

Cheryl stood in the doorway looking from one to the other. Howard wanted him to stay so badly he was fidgeting. David didn't want to. He looked extremely uncomfortable. She retreated into the kitchen.

"You show up out of the blue after all this time and can't even stay?"

"I wish I could, only I've got to make Pittsburgh tonight. I've an early flight out of Kennedy Airport for England, day after tomorrow."

He looked away from Howard's disappointment. Bad, bad mistake, stopping by. Neither expected him, they had no idea he was even in Ohio, why had he stopped? Being so close, how could he not? So here he was, "home" again. They'd talk further. Soon he'd start looking at the clock on the mantel, he'd fidget, he'd remind Howard how tight his schedule was—an excuse to get away—but not soon enough, not before the old wounds reopened. Hers and his own. He should have stayed on Route 70 and driven right by the turn-off.

Only he had to see her . . .

"Still with the religion?" Howard asked.

"Still."

"You teach it . . ."

He repeated what he had told Cheryl earlier. Howard tried again to feign interest. Should his need to surprise him? Howard had never approved of his career choice. He'd never given up hope that he'd eventually change his mind and take the job. If he only knew, in thirty years Great Lakes Re had never even entered his mind.

"You must like it to stick with it this long," Howard continued, "though you still should have come on board."

"Howard . . ." Busy in the kitchen, Cheryl rolled her eyes at the ceiling.

"I mean it, you made a goddamn mistake. A doozy. You'd be making a fortune today. The salaries and bonuses they're paying these days are out-of-sight."

"So I hear," said David.

"I see you still don't swear. Good for you."

There was an unwieldly pause. He sat leaning forward aimlessly fingering his beard. It felt like it was getting hotter in the room. Howard was upset. Over the job? After all these years? Cheryl reappeared in the doorway.

"Thirty years and you still haven't caught on, dear. Money doesn't interest him."

"Bullshit, money interests everybody. Tell me one man you know who's not interested in turning a buck."

David smiled. "How about Jesus?"

"Whoa, whoa, you hear this, Cheryl? Help me out here. Are you comparing yourself to Jesus Christ?" Cheryl laughed from the kitchen. Howard pressed on. "I see, you're pulling my leg. Besides, that's really far back, there was no capitalism back then, not much, anyway."

"Not like today," agreed David. "You can say one thing for back then, people took religion more seriously."

"Lots of people take religion seriously today. You don't exactly have a corner on commitment."

"I don't claim to, Howard." A pause. "Cheryl went back to work after I left."

Howard nodded, grateful for the change of subject. "For about ten years. She saved her money, I pitched in a little and she bought Thompson's Music Store. It's now Joyner Music, you must have seen it driving through."

"I must have missed it."

"It's a gold mine. She's got four people working for her, she just goes in now and then these days. Too busy for business, she works full time for charities, raising money for the Domestic Violence Service people, for United Cerebral Palsy, the Rain forest Foundation. She's got another recital coming up at the Civic Center in Columbus for the Palsy bunch. They've already sold close to three-thousand tickets. She plays all over . . ."

Cheryl returned setting the tray of drinks and cake on the cocktail table. She sat opposite them.

"She got to be quite a public speaker, too," Howard went on.

She smiled. "Amazing, isn't it? The mouse that roars."

"She's being modest, she's a real pro. You should hear her."

"Howard . . ."

"It all started after you left. She packed away the old Cheryl and trotted out a brand new one."

"Try the cake, David."

"She keeps me on my toes."

David picked at his cake, sipped his coffee and glanced at the clock five times by her count. After the hesitant and awkward beginning the two of them had gotten onto tracks and moved along smoothly, now would it fall apart?

"Are you married?" Howard asked.

"No."

Silence.

"I get the feeling you move around a lot. Do you move around a lot?"

"A lot."

Again, silence. It was like the room was holding its breath. She turned her glass in her hand for something to do. After the opening barrage of questions and answers they'd used up what they had to talk about. Reminiscence became forced, Howard began repeating himself. To go on raking over old ground seemed pointless, and there was the risk that either she or David might touch on something better left to memory.

He seemed lonely. Moving about as he did he probably had few friends, no close friends. Writing was lonely work.

He had never been outgoing, not compared to Howard, but he was more outgoing than he was showing at the moment. It reached a point where the clock's ticking sounded like hammer blows. Conversation became sparser. The gaps became glaring, the clock louder. David finally set down his glass, clapped his hands on his knees and stood up.

"I really should get along."

"You haven't been here an hour yet," Howard complained. "You haven't seen my telescope. You pop in, right out again. After this long?"

"I'm sorry."

"I know, you keep saying that. Oh hell, listen to me, I'm disappointed so I get annoyed. I'm the one who should be apologizing."

They went outside. It was getting cooler and the air less humid. He got behind the wheel of the jeep.

"Boy, this thing's seen better days," said Howard. "Not much tread left on those tires. I hope you make it to New York. Could you use some money?"

"Howard . . . !"

"Just asking, what's wrong with that? How about it, Dave?"

"I'm okay, thanks anyway." He was looking at their car in the driveway. "Beauty. It looks brand new."

"A month old," beamed Howard. "Japanese, drives like a dream. Well, I guess this is it. For another thirty years." He laughed. Neither of them could manage even a smile. "Drive carefully. You remember how to get back onto Route 70?"

"Yes. Good-bye. Good-bye, Cheryl, have a good life. Both of you. It was great seeing you both again."

Have a good life, his final words before dusting off on the Harley, before she boarded the bus back to Columbus. She set a hand on his shoulder and leaned over. He offered his cheek, she kissed it. Howard pumped his hand. He started the engine, footing the gas.

"I'll send you a postcard from Cambridge."

"That'll be a first," Howard admonished him.

They waved and watched as he made a U-turn and drove off, disappearing around the corner. Inside, she collected the cake plates and glasses. David had barely tasted his cake and coffee. She carried the tray to the kitchen. Together they rinsed the glasses and dishes for the dishwasher.

"Out of the blue and back into it," murmured Howard. "And I couldn't get in two words about the job."

"With Great Lakes? Are you serious? Howard, he's in his fifties . . ."

"And no more interested than the man in the moon, I know, but he's still as sharp as ever, he'd be an asset. If we're in touch when he gets back from England, he may be interested. Of course he'd have to shave and cut six inches off his hair."

"Are you listening to yourself?"

"I know, I know, he's too old, I'm reaching." He paused. "Did you notice how he looked at you?" He laughed. "About the same way you looked at him."

"What are you talking about?"

He set the last rinsed dish in the dishwasher, straightened up and eyed her somberly. "Sweetheart, I may not be the most perceptive man on the block but I'm not stone blind. Think back, remember that afternoon he drove me home from the airport? It was the day I took you up to the observatory to look at Mercury. As soon as I got into the car beside him I could see he was nervous. All the way home he talked about how disappointed he was with OSU, but that was just a cover to avoid talking about what was really on his mind. I couldn't figure out what was going on until we walked into the house and you started behaving the same way. It hit me."

She turned from the sink to avoid his eyes, feeling suddenly desperate and ashamed. His restrained tone of voice put her on edge—if only he'd explode, berate her.

"You never said . . ."

"What would you have wanted me to say? Should I have lit into you both? Accused? Threatened? What good would that have done any of us?"

"You knew all this time . . ."

"I suppose I could have blown up. I sure felt like it. I could have said something really nasty, driven you right out the door."

She covered her face with her hands, shaking her head.

"Take it easy. I didn't, did I? I thought it over and decided that apart from everything else it was a test. You'd either run off with him or he'd leave. I was lucky, it worked out the way I hoped it would."

"Howard . . ."

"And we've gotten through all these years without a sword hanging over our heads. I didn't say anything for another reason, the most important one. Because I love you. I could never hurt you, not in retaliation, not any way."

"I had it coming . . ."

"No. It was a mistake, that's all. People trip, it's only human. I think I knew all along if I didn't tamper, it would straighten itself out. I've always been a little short on confidence. Always worried a little bit about being so much older. Still, I've always had delusions of adequacy."

"Don't! Don't ever say that. You're a wonderful husband. I love you!" He held her. She hugged him close. "There's something else. I should have told you back then but I didn't have the courage. Howard . . ." She sighed. "I left with him . . ."

He held her from him. In his eyes was no surprise, no anger, no puzzlement, only love. In that instant she treasured him.

"I had a hunch you did," he murmured. "But you came back, which was the same as if you'd never left, right? And we've been happy all these years. No dredging it up when we disagree about something else. No bitterness, no sword. We've been happy."

"Very."

"No grudges, no regrets. It's dead and buried."

With the added glasses and plates, the dishwasher was now fully loaded. He closed the door and turned it on.

"Poor Dave, he couldn't get out of here fast enough. You think, even after all this time, it's still on his conscious? I hope not." He glanced at the clock. "It's getting late, I should finish up that door. It should only take an hour. How about giving me a hand?"

"You don't need one."

"No, but you're welcome to kibitz."

"Would you mind if I went for a walk instead?"

"Sure." He studied her. "You okay? I'm a little shaken, you must be too."

"I'm okay now. I won't be long." She kissed him.

"That was nice, can I have another?"

She kissed him again. "I love you, Howard. Always."

"For better or worse forever, that's us."

She could hear him singing on his way to the rear of the house. Outside, she thought about what David had said, about her being the only rose in his garden. She recalled coming home on her birthday to find the roses strewn all over the piano. She thought how close they came, but only close, and she could honestly say she never regretted staying and weathering the storm in her heart.

175

She crossed the lawn to the car in the driveway. She set her hand against it. Magically, it became the old car on that morning, the morning they'd had the water fight and how embarrassed she'd felt when she discovered he could see through her dress where the hose had soaked her. It seemed scandalous thinking about it in the shower afterward. Only the years reduced it to innocence, as had the feeling sweeping through her when she stood close to him looking at *Luncheon on the Grass*, at the Manet exhibit.

At the end of the street she took the path into the woods. Birds sang. A warbler, its wings chevroned, its throat and breast yellow, hopped from branch to branch trailing a somewhat melancholy trill. It suited her mood. It was cooler among the trees. Bluish-purple lupins crowded the base of the oak; early-blooming hepaticas still lingered, flaunting their purple, blue and white blossoms.

The woods on either side of the path had thickened to near-impenetrability since Howard brought her here the first time to show her the table. It came into view in the glade, as immutable and ageless as the trees overlording it. There wasn't a square inch on its surface that wasn't gouged or carved. It was still serviceable, although slightly rickety under the occasional jug of lemonade or picnic basket, coolers, cups, elbows.

A light breeze feathered through the trees and the birds vied with each other, opening their hearts in song. David sat opposite, the textbook he'd been highlighting between them. His gravity gave him away; she knew what was coming: Clive Holbrook, the patrol, all the Vietnam memories that fed and fattened his guilt. His eyes said opening up would not be easy, and he spared himself not at all. She listened, she disagreed, for his every argument she had a counter argument but, not surprisingly, she couldn't get through. Logic, common sense had no value to him that afternoon. He didn't want her to change his mind about anything, he wanted an ear and a nod. They'd nearly gotten into an argument.

By then he'd come a long way toward readjusting since arriving home with Angela, but that afternoon proved that he still had a long way to go, and with Angela gone she would have to be the one to help him. She was willing. Too willing? And failed to realize that another factor was at work: already, she was falling in love. She'd been so confident, so sure of maintaining control, she actually thought she could help without becoming emotionally involved. Or did she see the danger and ignore it? It was hard to remember.

She wished him happiness. If that wasn't to be, at least contentment. He seemed satisfied with his life, only all this roaming about, his restlessness, hinted that he was still searching. Would she have made a difference?

She heard voices, children coming up the path. She looked up at the beech tree behind David and opposite her. It had nearly doubled in size since the day they had sat there. The children were closer. She could hear a man's voice calling them. A family picnic. She got up and walked around behind the beech.

There was a heart around a D and C with a smaller heart joining them. She had come the day after he left for New Mexico to look at it. Back then the freshly cut wood was white. Gradually, the years had made their heart as much a part of the tree as any burl or branch. It seemed to wear David's handiwork proudly, like a badge of honor: private and personal pronouncement of their love. The day after she came to see it, her final day at the library, she looked up beech trees in one of the encyclopedias and found that some species live as long as four hundred years.

She touched his initial, touched her own, set her palm

against the heart and looked straight up through the branches. *You hold this heart in trust, guard and preserve it.*

The family had arrived at the table. She could hear talking as they set out their food and utensils. She edged to her right into the brush to avoid being seen. It was very thick, and she wished she had a machete to cut her way through. She made it to the path and started for home.

Author Biography

Barbara Riefe, born December 21, 1945 in Prospect, Connecticut, is the author of twenty-three novels. THIS RAVAGED HEART appeared on the New York Times best-seller list and altogether, ten of her romances combined to sell over 4,000,000 copies, THIS RAVAGED HEART leading the way at 780,000.

Barbara lives with her husband, Alan, the writer, in Wilton, Connecticut and is currently working on a romance, tentatively titled: WHAT ARE FRIENDS FOR? They are the parents of four children and have four grandchildren.

Her most recent books deal with women making the trek westward in the mid-nineteenth century. Entitled: DESPERATE CROSSING, AGAINST ALL ODDS and WOMEN WEST, they are written from the woman's point of view. Said Publisher's Weekly of DESPERATE CROSSING, "Riefe tells her story with action-packed verve and satisfying detail," and went on to praise both plot and dialogue. Said Booklist of the same book, "Tension coupled with graphic historical detail makes this a novel difficult to put down."